I0460389

DEVOTED

Part 4

Affairs of the Heart Series ~ London

KEW TOWNSEND

Tremmelle Publishing

HOLLYWOOD, CALIFORNIA

© 1993, 2011, 2016 by KEW Townsend

DISCLAIMER: ***DEVOTED*** is **PART 4** in the *Affairs of the Heart Series-London.* It is a strong "adult" themed work of fiction. This book is not for readers under the age of 18 or has difficulty with CLIFFHANGER ENDINGS. This title was previously published as *Heart of the Hurri-Kaine.*

Publishers Note: Names, characters, places, and incidents are products of the author's imagination and are used fictitiously. Any resemblance to actual events, locales, or persons, living or dead, is entirely coincidental.

All rights reserved as permitted under the U. S. Copyright Act of 1976, Berne Copyright Convention, Universal Copyright Convention, and Pan-American Copyright Convention. No part of this book may be reproduced, or transmitted in any form, or by any means, including downloading to an unauthorized site (defined as a site not recognized by the author) by PDF or any digital form, photocopying, or electronic or mechanical, including shareware, recording, or by any information storage or stored in retrieval systems, without permission, in writing from the author, at
http://kewtownsend.com

Author acknowledges the copyright or trademarked status and trademark owners of the following wordmarks mention in this work of fiction — Levi's, Hard Rock Café, Bentley, Cristal Champagne, Dodger Blue, Prada — All chapter headings using song titles and the musician names associated with them.

© 2016 Tremmelle Publishing, United States
© 2015 Cover Design by Sparkle Graphics
© 2015 Cover Layout by Jesse Kimmel-Freeman
© 2015 Cover images by RefleXtion; By-Studio
© 2014 Book Layout BookDesignTemplates.com

Sign up for NEWSLETTER at www.kewtownsend.com

PROMISES/ KEW Townsend
ISBN 978– 06925006-1-3

Affairs of the Heart Series
London

HEART (Part 1)
TEMPTATION (Part 2)
PROMISES (Part 3)

Forthcoming
BETRAYAL (Part 5)

Sign up for NEWSLETTER

kewtownsend.com

Dedication

To "Young Guitar Players," acting like a gunslinger.
For my husband Boyd, that passed away too soon, a gifted songwriter that pulled magic words out of the air in the style of Bob Dylan, his hero.

CONTENTS

Chapter One

TODAY

1989

London, England

Day 4

H olly Hill lived in a fairy tale world with her rock star prince, Kaine Walker. He was a magnificent man to love. But most importantly, he loved her too. She leaned into Kaine, squeezing him extra hard to make sure the forbidden fruit wasn't an impossible dream.

The ride into London became super uncomfortable. Straddling the back of the motorized horse, each bump or dip in the road hurt Holly, especially after making powerful love for hours at Briarwood Castle, with Kaine, her energetic and dedicated rock star lover. But Holly's spirits were high. She would enter the bustling city on the fourth day of this incredible adventure and all facets of her life had changed.

Right on cue, the next face to pop into her mind was Luka Hunter the Cable Music Television (CMT) representative, with his beautiful blue angel eyes. She hoped her choice to commit to a forever love with Kaine would cool Luka's heated and frequent advances since he was simply impossible to resist.

She thought of her parents, her editor father Arthur, and stay–at–home mother, Anne. How would they react to Kaine Walker, Rock Star? As the frontman for the world famous rock band *Hurrikaine*, her music loving father, would adore him. Her sensible mother would worry, as usual. One way to distract her mother would be to give her the grandchildren she waited to spoil, and that Kaine had pleaded with her to have with him. But what would they think about Kaine, the most famous rock star of his time, as the father of her children?

She was not that short sighted to realize that marrying Kaine was to marry an empire. It boggled her mind to guess how much his financial holdings would be, perhaps millions of dollars. Hadn't Kaine said hundreds of millions? If his attorneys were any good, they would insist on a crippling prenuptial agreement, and why not. Protecting Kaine was sound business.

Wait, was she thinking about marrying Kaine Walker, the most famous rock star of her time?

"My how things have changed." She accepted with a purr while the motorcycle's engine drowned out her voice. She shook her head clear. Then again, in a few days, she and Luka

Hunter would be in L.A., and they could be friends while Kaine was away on the European leg of the eighteen months worldwide tour.

No, bad idea, such a bad idea!

The lush English countryside faded into tall, brick-stained buildings while the sky remained clear and the breeze crisp.

Kaine yelled over his shoulder. "I need to make a stop. You mind?"

"Whatever you want," she answered.

"I'm taking you to London's hip, Notting Hill Gate district. I think you'll like it."

He parked the bike on a busy, colorful street that looked like pictures of the Sixties Mod movement. He pointed with a glance.

"This is the original Asset boutique."

The second Kaine hit the doorway, Holly experienced her first taste as girlfriend to the famous Kaine. The difference from one moment to the next was instant. Heads turned, eyes pinned them and tongues wagged, all followed by whispers. Holly noted this response was more overwhelming than Brett's popularity in L.A., at the height of the Collins murder trial.

The atmosphere was different as if a mysterious spell shrouded the room. Kaine the rock star had arrived, and they all knew his history better than she did. She wandered over to the leather section where her handsome Kaine stood trying on a dark jacket.

"They had a problem with the fit of the shoulders. I wanted it finished in time for tonight. What do you think?"

Holly walked up behind him. She slipped her arms around his waist, went up on her tiptoes, and whispered in his ear. "I think … I want you inside me." She leaned into him and he responded by kissing her deeply. She kissed him back, wrapping her leg around his for the entire world to see.

"I'll buy a thousand jackets if I can count on this reaction every time I wear one," he confirmed his voice smoky and ready for love. A tiny laugh followed his words. "I will wear this tonight, for you."

"What is tonight?"

"Last night at Wembley Arena. This afternoon I have a sound check, three interviews, and Luka wants to film segments of the sound check for CMT. We have a full day."

"We?"

"You will come with me, won't you?" he said as his voice rose in a panic, then let go of her and stood back.

"Why, yes, of course. I didn't have the itinerary."

"Smashing! What do you think of this?" He whirled around gracefully posing like a runway model.

"I think I see why you drive the girl's c-r-a-z-y like you do me," she joked and then pretended to faint in his arms.

"Will that bother you?" he asked in a serious tone, searching her eyes for the truth.

"No, I know who has your heart."

Kaine grabbed her hand and squeezed it in agreement. "I love *you*, Miss Holly Hill, never forget that." And he took an extra-long moment to stare into her eyes.

"Did you find something you liked, sir?" Interrupted the sales clerk, obviously impressed he was waiting on the globetrotting Kaine.

Kaine stopped and exhaled a weary sigh. "This should be it. Add the waistcoat and anything the lady's selected. Express it to my hotel right away." He handed the boy a piece of paper where he'd written the name of his hotel.

"What did you select Miss?"

"I haven't selected anything!" She declared. She'd misread Kaine's instructions. He'd meant for her to shop too.

"We have a little time. Let's have a look." Kaine directed after he had changed his jacket. He took her by the hand, leading her to another section. He picked out a short, black, lace dress with purple, satin, piping to match his jacket.

She stepped into the dressing area and checked the price. Her jaw dropped. She couldn't pay for this.

Kaine peeked between the curtains.

"Why haven't you tried it on, My Lady?"

"Kaine, I can't possibly afford this. I can't even afford the thread."

"I said I'd take care of you, provide for you. Please, let me keep my word."

"But Kaine, I can't. I have no way to show you, my love, this way."

In a matter-of-fact tone, he explained. "It's only money, Holly. And you my love have given me what money can't possibly buy, a bright, new future with you."

A moment later Kaine returned with more gorgeous, and expensive, dresses for her. Eventually, Holly stepped from the room completely dressed in his latest choice. She became convinced that she was born to wear Asset.

"That's it. Let's take them." He stated.

"These pieces cost a small fortune," she argued too loud.

"You look smashing." He praised and then kissed her neck to convince her and for all to see.

"Please, allow me to keep my promise to you. Let me show My Lady, how happy you've made me. Let me spoil you," he whispered near her ear, in a tone of please don't argue with me. The staff busied themselves attending to Kaine's stacks of procurements. Everyone catered to him and seemed to want to show him how much they adored him. He graciously signed autographs for all who asked and posed for photographs, taking the time to speak with each person as if he had a personal interest in them. Kaine was indeed an unusual man, a man of the people.

A swelling sense of pride washed over her. She began to realize what it meant to be his girlfriend. She smiled a broad grin as he took her hand and walked out the door, leaving every woman in the store envious of her.

Kaine scanned the street and led her into an elegant jewelry store. The clerk addressed him by his surname.

Everyone knew Kaine.

Holly bent over the glass case, admiring all the expensive necklaces and bracelets.

Kaine said, "I've always wanted to pierce my ear. Why don't we do it together? It would be a symbol of our new life and commitment to each other."

She smiled at him. "Kaine Walker! You're a hopeless romantic."

Happy with her response, he petitioned the jeweler behind the counter. "I like this," pointing to a simple gold hooped earring. "Make that a pair of hoops," he added and smiled knowingly at her.

Chapter Two

FEEL LIKE MAKING LOVE

aine started the bike causing a commotion on the street, simply because he was Kaine. He stopped at a restaurant and again, everyone scrutinized Holly as Kaine entered the eatery. People arrived from nowhere to surround him. After a few moments, she realized she could never focus on her light lunch. She pushed aside the beef barley soup, grilled cheese sandwich, and ice tea because the long line of requests for autographs and photo opportunities had begun. When she climbed onto the back of the motorbike, she'd had a different perception of Kaine Walker's life.

"I've had your purchases sent to the hotel. We should stop at yours and collect all your belongings."

"Why?"

"You're my girlfriend, and where I come from girlfriends live with me. Any objections?" He was asking her, but the stern look in his eyes said that was that!

They parked at her hotel to collect her few personal items.

Inside her room, she handed papers to him.

"Kaine, what do I do with this stack of messages? Most

are from tabloids. They want pictures and interviews of me. There are seven from Brett, and he doesn't sound happy. I think the news of you and I have reached the states."

"What are you going to do?" he asked while sitting on the settee with his legs crossed, thumbing through a paperback book in a vampire series.

"I have a plan. I'll call Brett and tell the truth. I've met a magnificent man and we are in love. Therefore, I'm calling off the engagement."

What else could she do?

Kaine sat up, put the book down, and strolled over to her. He took Brett's messages out of her hand and dropped them into the wastebasket, the others he stuffed into his leather satchel.

"Brett will have to learn to wait for you. I'll give these to Luka. He'll have the best way to handle them."

"It's begun, hasn't it, Kaine?" She acknowledged the sharp twist in her stomach.

"Yes, My Lady. Welcome to the Eye of the *Hurrikaine*. Expect Luka to brief you on security policies, perhaps assign you a bodyguard."

"Do you think that is necessary?"

"You will find out soon enough that little depends on what I think. Luka runs the show. He always has. I'm only the king pawn moved about where needed. Meant to stimulate publicity, generate ticket sales, and sell records," he complained as his voice ran flat and joyless.

"Why do you stay in this line of work if it makes you unhappy?"

"It's difficult to understand from your position. You see all the restrictions and limitations. Unfortunately, you will never experience the payoff."

"And what is the payoff?"

"To perform is the best experience in the world."

"The best?" She couldn't stop her soaring spirits from taking a dip.

"Better than anything I've ever experienced with sex, drugs, fame or any professional recognition. To perform is worth all the hassles when I step onto that stage. Nothing can beat it."

"Then my only rival for your love is music."

Kaine was quiet. Then spoke barely above a whisper.

"I've never had to choose." He threw back his head and ran his fingers down his long, shiny hair then draped a long lock behind his ear. "Hope I never have to, My Lady," he stated pointedly glancing at her as his voice cooled with an edge. His usually dreamy eyes were cold and emotionless.

She wasn't brave enough to ask his choice.

A half hour later Holly was relaxing in her new home, the penthouse of the Lainesbough Hotel, well under Kaine's charming spell. He'd carried her to his bed, stripped her, then himself. Kaine protected his strong love and seconds later, he was pumping high inside her. Their syncopated sighs of pleasure filled his room where he no longer slept alone.

Holly squeezed her legs around him tight while he moved in and out of her and whispered, "I love you." She no longer wondered where he stopped and she began.

Moments later, while holding him deep inside, his body shaking from his release, she ran her fingers through his long, damp hair. She gazed into his sparkling, blue eyes as her fingertips traced the line of his hair across the shape of his dreamy eyes, down along the hollow of his cheek where she pressed her lips to his. She tenderly kissed and stroked him lightly until his cold, harsh, world blasted in once again with a volley of phone calls. Though they'd interrupted their passion, Kaine patiently answered all.

"Yes, I'm getting ready."

"Yes, I'm ready for the sound check at Wembley."

"Yes, I have everything I need." He insisted, throwing a satisfied look to Holly making her all warm and fuzzy.

"Yes, yes, yes."

A half hour later he stood showered and dressed in fitted black Levi's, a loose, light-purple *Hurrikaine* tour shirt that read *Illusions of Self* across his chest and a beat-up, black leather, *Hurrikaine* flight-jacket. His face was clean-shaven, his dark, wet hair pulled back into a tail. The exotic scent of his exclusive cologne traveled quickly to remind her how intoxicating he could be. He was always handsome and never seemed to experience a bad look. Another hot flash stirred deep below her belly.

Kaine headed toward her standing and waiting for him. His cologne flooded her senses continuing to knock her off balance. He slipped his cool hands inside the terrycloth robe.

"Mmmm," she whispered enjoying his hands warming her as they freely roamed her naked body. One stopped over the flatness of her stomach, then on down to cover her finding her wet with desire for him. His fingers slipped inside her as Holly lifted her leg and wrapped it around his thigh. Deeper he moved in and out of her. His thumb rubbed the bud of her ecstasy perfectly, forcing her to lose count of the endless waves of pleasure. His touch left her dizzy and wanting him. She barely heard his invitation whispered between strings of moist, passionate kisses.

When Kaine drew a breath to separate from her, he asked.

"Are you sure you won't come with me to Wembley for the sound check? It's private. More fun than the actual concert." He enticed, trying to lure her as he continued to touch her in places she'd remember forever.

"Yes." She firmly agreed between shallow pants. "It's clear that I need rest if I'm going to keep up with my handsome, sexy, man tonight." She wisely confessed. She stroked his face before dropping kisses on the ridge of his neck surprised she could refuse him anything. But she couldn't speak any longer, she couldn't think any longer because Kaine had expressed her back to the magical place. His fingers were moving faster as she pulled his head down and kissed him as she exploded in his arms.

Kaine held her tight because she'd lost her strength to stand. How quickly Kaine's skilled fingers brought her explosive pleasure. Kaine kissed her cocking his head one way and then the other until she gained her balance and let her limp leg slide down his to the floor.

He tilted his head to one side. "How did I get so lucky? All of London is demanding an invitation to our exclusive sound check. But here you are My Lady, content to sleep and wait for me while I go to work. Feels provincial," he said with a twist of a laugh.

He hesitated and added, "I miss you already My Lady, but I will take the essence of you with me."

He pulled his fingers from inside her and placed them in

his mouth.

His words shocked her, but not as much as his action. Before she thought or spoke another word, Kaine pulled his fingers from his lips and kissed her deeply, leaving no space in the cavern of her mouth untouched. Only the soft scent of her own body punctuated the steamy kiss. That changed her mind about the sound check and was about to inform him when a hard, intrusive knock and yelling severed their private moment.

"Kaine! Let's go! We're late. Now!"

She stiffened in Kaine's arms, holding him as if a shield to the unknown. She had pulled one last kiss of strength from him before she released him. Her knees buckled as her stomach tightened like a knot in a rope.

Kaine noticed her anxiety and kissed her desperately as if he would never taste her lips again.

The message clear.

The voice is unmistakable.

Luka.

Chapter Three

YOU ARE THE SUNSHINE
OF MY LIFE

olly tried to smile and hide her anxiety. "It's all right Kaine, I'll be here. As you said, waiting for you until you're finished working."

Kaine's sweet, dreamy eyes conveyed it all, as relief smoothed his taut face. He yelled in the direction of the door.

"Meet you at the elevator."

Good move.

They were speaking to each other without words. Kaine quickly hugged her, grabbed his leather satchel and threw open the door. He turned in the doorway, looked at her one last time, sending shivers throughout her body. He took the fingers he had loved her with, placed them to his lips and blew her a kiss. Then he spun around on his heels and vanished, leaving her with a cold loneliness that chilled her like a winter storm.

Holly pulled the terry cloth robe tightly around her, pushed up the collar to bury her face, and deeply inhaled his cologne.

She popped in a Roberts blues CD, pushed repeat and decided what to do first. She needed a shower and sleep. Instead, Holly leaned against the window watching the Bentley enter traffic. She wondered if she'd made a giant mistake declining Kaine's invitation.

Good, she had a plan.

Time was needed to researching *Hurrikaine* and give a bit of attention to her grooming. She wanted to dress especial nice for Kaine tonight. However, she needed answers to the Kaine and Luka mystery. That would take more time. For the moment, she wandered into their bedroom. She was tired, drained. She altered her plan for a few minutes rest.

A fresh, black Hurrikaine T-shirt that read *Lose Your Illusions* lay on the floor. She dropped the robe and pulled it over her love-ravaged body then sank deep, down under the toasty gold duvet. She promised herself catnap, that's all. She rolled away from the side of the sheets that were damp from their unrestrained lovemaking, missing him, thinking about how she'd ended up in his bed, his girlfriend.

Three days ago, the rock band Hurrikaine hadn't meant anything to her other than a few old love songs that had topped the late 70s and early 80s charts. Rock music had been far from her staid life. Especially, as an investigator for her childhood friend's law firm in Beverly Hills, California.

A childhood friend was an unfair characterization of Brett Templeton or was it an exact description of their current relationship? Brett saved her seven years ago from certain tragedy. He waited patiently for her to set a marriage date — one that wouldn't arrive.

Three days ago, she'd met the most beautiful man she'd

ever seen.

Yes, Luka Hunter was amazing. Tall and blond with dark blue eyes she'd once thought she'd die for, yes, Luka. He'd been sent to lead her through the tremulous valley of rock 'n' roll and brought new hope for a love affair.

Luka had protected her from the low life rockers and guttersnipe groupies and especially away from a particular womanizing rocker. But he couldn't protect her from the rock star that had entered her life out of a mist in a music video and delivered the special romantic kiss that had awakened her heart. Kaine Walker, tall, dark, and so handsome, a romantic time traveler that had swept her off her feet, stealing her away from the always beautiful Luka.

The paparazzi caught her and Kaine kissing in front of Buckingham Palace. The photograph, plastered all over the covers of the tabloids and London press, insinuated Kaine Walker had a secret girlfriend. That had placed them in this tenuous circumstance, beyond their control. Kaine asked her if after one date, did she want to be known as his girlfriend, or to walk away while she could.

The only sensible answer was to ask Kaine to show her how to love him and make his life better. He'd been happy because he had been such a lonely man. Then he made her dreams come true and gave her the fairy tale, with all the trimmings, by taking her with him to shoot the last of the music video.

It was there, at a fairy tale castle, Kaine pulled out all the stops. The only problem and it had been a big one, was to face Luka. He hadn't taken the change in programming well. No, he'd come after her, but she'd stood steadfast and committed to

Kaine. And though she was a stranger to both of them, in this complicated predicament, Kaine became her boyfriend.

But Kaine had been clear. Luka wouldn't care. It was a matter of time before he'd come for her. That was when she and Kaine made a pack to stay together vowing never to allow Luka to tear them apart.

She smiled, remembering the long night and early morning of making love with Kaine. How he had stopped the sun from shining as a sign of his invincible love for her. They'd left the fairy tale castle to return to London a few hours earlier and he'd moved her in with him.

Life was perfect.

Chapter Four

TAKE IT TO THE LIMIT

How long Holly slept was an unknown. She was dreaming of Kaine and the castle when every labored breath she inhaled stank of rancid liquor. Next, the warm comforter was torn from her body. The cold air covered her, along with a blanket of fear before she opened her eyes. Her anxiety rose quickly.

Someone drug the T-shirt up and it became tangled in her hair while pulling it over her head, inviting the cold of the night shadows to settle over her sensitive nipples making them hardened instantly like seed shells. Blinded by inky darkness, with her arms and hair tangled up in the shirt she shivered as she fought to distinguish this moment from a nightmare.

Was this real?

She tried to recognize each slurred word.

"Baby, Baby, I missed you so much." The voice repeated in an unrecognizable tone.

The mouth slammed down on her taking her by surprise. This couldn't be Luka. Or, did he double back, with Kaine trapped for hours at the sound check? Security would have prevented any other man than Luka to enter Kaine's suite. Would Luka do this? Or, was this the payoff? Her body had been saying yes and Luka was sooo human.

Unable to reduce the fear that saturated her mind, she stiffened. No suitable defense against the intruder came to mind. Her heart raced. She strained to see into the darkness as the cloth ripped above her head.

Everything moved too fast. She tried to identify the intruder.

The kiss and the rough movements were not of her sweet, tender Kaine. If this was Luka, he too was different, and she had to stop him, quickly before he made a horrible mistake. The heavy weight of the presence pinned her down against any will she had to move. His mouth closed over hers before she could protest. He continued to hold her arms above her head as his legs straddled her thighs. He sent one message — he was stronger and would take what he wanted.

Who was this intruder?

He pulled his stinking mouth away from her long enough to tell her.

"Baby, I missed your sweet..." he'd slurred into nothingness.

To cut him off she squirmed, trying to free herself. His lips came crashing down again, his tongue filling her mouth, siphoning her words, as she struggled. In her disoriented state, she attempted to fight him. Before she moved his slobbery mouth from hers, he moved down her body bringing her hands with him.

Holly gasped for air and then filled with anxiety, waiting to see if he would stop. She wondered which moment she should scream out to alert security. In the next moment, his wet lips surrounded her breast and the hard edge of his teeth nipped at the sensitive skin of her nipple.

She tried to scream out the words trapped in her mind, to rebuke him as she fought.

"Luka stop!"

Instead, the man moved back up and covered her lips. He crushed her mouth with his, swallowing her cries. He forced her teeth to cut into the flesh of her lip. The salty taste of her blood trickled into her mouth, followed by his aggressive, serpent-like tongue.

Her struggle to be free only served to excite him further. To fight was in vain. He outweighed her, outmaneuvered her, yet Holly fought his kiss, biting his lips, attempting to speak when his damp hair fell upon her face.

To her horror, her body betrayed her, falling into a rhythm with the intruders. Apparently, her yielding motion aroused the intruder more. And too late, her body wanted to desire him in a shameless way. But her mind and spirit didn't want him this way.

He burrowed his strong, clothed body between her legs. His bent knees pushed her thighs apart beyond their natural intent. She ached from his rugged touch. His hands, hot and robust hands, dominated her. His hands demanding to roam up and down her naked body, over, around, in and out of her body. Skilled fingers that left her helpless under his powerful touch. She hated him for making her body send waves of undeniable pleasure as his fingers plunged sinfully inside her again and again.

Holly stopped her struggle to untangle herself from him,

understanding the results he sought, no longer fearing what would happen. She couldn't stop him because of his powerful hunger and superhuman strength. Luka would take all of her, anyway, he wanted her, and soon.

Holly's concerns drained quickly.

He threw his head down beside hers, his cheek brushing hers, his damp hair on her face. It was then she caught the faint scent of cologne. She knew who this was. But she didn't understand why?

She completely surrendered her body and spirit.

His fiery body ignited quickly spreading into a raging passion. His fingers pumped her as the groans of pleasure rapidly poured from his lips. Then he plunged his fingers higher and harder into her, this man was undeniable — he was Kaine.

Kaine shifted his weight, unevenly, crushing her beneath him. He groped for his pants to free himself. Kaine's poet's words were in her ear, private, words of sex, liberally describing pictures of things he wanted to do with her body. He intended to live out his fantasies as he pressed hard against her. He anxiously jabbed at her, missing, sending waves of pain between her upper thighs.

She wasn't ready and tried to move to adapt to him under his crushing lips. She frantically ran her hand over his jacket while inhaling the scent of his leather. Her fingers were groping him, struggling to pull him off her.

He ignored her pleas, her hands — he wouldn't stop. She slipped her hands up under his jacket and dove under his T-shirt to touch his hot skin. There, she dug into his flesh, dragging her long fingernails down his hot, wet skin, as he rammed inside her, sinking deeper.

Holly screamed out into his mouth. The stabbing pain caused her to lurch, hitting her head against the headboard. His burning lips and slippery tongue devoured her, swallowing her cries, rendering her mute. He lunged harder and harder. And when she screamed a muffled cry, she dug deeper into his flesh dragging her nails the full length of his back.

"What the fuck?" He screamed out, arching his upper torso like a wolf howling at the moon. He released her mouth for only a moment, caught a breath, but he did not stop plunging inside her.

On the contrary, her wildcat reaction urged him on, believing she wanted his rough touch.

Kaine plunged deeper and deeper with each thrust, bringing more excitement for him than the last. His groans more frequent, harder, faster, lost in an uncontrollable firestorm. He placed his hands on each side of her shoulders, raising his torso to force his hardness, and plunged again, dropping deep, so deep, searching for the bliss that awaited him high inside her.

She twisted her hips under him, moving to accept all his hard, long form as he thrust into her, trying to go higher than physically allowed.

He groaned so deep inside his chest, she would have once taken pride in his satisfaction, but not this time. She barely made out the pleasured expression pouring forth to cloak his face. His eyes closed, lost in her — ignoring her sighs of protest.

Kaine relaxed in her sweaty, limp body. He stretched her arms straight out crucifixion style, holding her wrist, pinning her. He had vanished in the pleasure, the lust, and complete abandon of fucking her. He plunged into her with long hard strokes. Disgust filled her mind as the grunts of pleasure and delight escaped from her own lips.

How could she urge him to continue? Why convince him she was having a wonderful time? She hoped the act would end soon. But it didn't. There was the sound of her heavy pant, the movement of her hips in sync with his.

He peaked, gasped, and his body became streamlined as he collapsed onto her body. He placed his lips next to her ear, promising her the world. And although every nerve in her body pulsated, she lay still ... so still. All that passed between them was the warmth of his seed until he was empty.

"Kaine..." she sighed.

She was unprepared for this Kaine. He was wild, demanding and scared the hell out of her. It sounded romantic to think she wanted her man to make mad passionate and violent love to her. But when it happened, it was not romantic — it was degrading.

Kaine slowly withdrew his shrinking desire, rolled to her side and stretched out his lean physique.

She quickly wrapped her body around the corner of the sheet.

Their breaths slowed.

Between exhaling deep puffs, he faintly begged.

"Lady, never ... ever ... leave me."

Holly lay quietly. Her face dripping with his sweat, and for the life of her, she didn't have anything to say to him. For the moment, she stifled the urge to get up and run far away.

"You make me incredibly happy, I love having you with

me." He sweetly confessed.

Beautiful words were mixed with a faint groan in her ear. His breath, hot, laced with foul smelling liquor. She lay listening to Roberts etch another moment in her memory with Kaine. One she'd as soon forget.

Kaine pulled the sheet off her, dropped his hand onto her sweaty body, enjoying himself as if she were served up to him on a platter for his enjoyment. His hand roamed generously, touching every inch of her he could reach as if he alone owned her.

Holly despised herself for accepting his caress, soothing her, calming her. His warm hand moved gracefully over and down her body. His fingers moved in and out of the wetness of her. He knew her body so well.

Holly finally spoke with a faint whisper into his ear.

"What got into you?"

She waited.

His hand came to rest cupping a breast. His lips moved to lick the swollen curve of her and then gently suckled her nipple, oblivious to her question.

Then, as quickly as the attack begun, it ended. Kaine moved, rose, and zipped up his pants.

In the dim spotlight of the moonbeam, she saw him stumble into the living room and switched on a lamp. In the swatch of light, she watched him pull off his jacket and throw it on the floor. He simply dismissed his cruel, new sexual appetite as if nothing out of the ordinary had happened between them.

What disturbed her most? The fact that he didn't think his sexual proclivities were unusual.

He'd traveled everywhere and as he had carefully pointed out, had countless women any way he'd wanted them. Perhaps this was her future with Kaine. Random sexual acts. A few with love, others with disrespect. She lay stationary on the bed like a deer caught in headlights. She watched Kaine pop open a beer, then drained it without stopping. It was the first alcohol she'd seen him drink. Something was different about Kaine, something more than this brutal episode.

There came a knock on the door. It distracted him. The knock grew louder and more insistent.

He answered and rudely commented. "About fucking time, here's for your trouble. Hey, counselor, our clothes are here. Those fuckers sure waited until the last moment. We have about an hour to get ready and get the fuck out of here." He blurted with such vulgarity into the darkness of the bedroom.

Holly watched Kaine intently as if on a surveillance stakeout. He threw the bagged garments worth tens of thousands of dollars, on a nearby chair and then like a wasted paper towel they slid to the floor.

The phone rang, and she propped herself up on one elbow to watch his every movement, completely puzzled by his behavior. He grabbed another beer and headed to answer the phone.

She chided herself for jumping to conclusions. Perhaps she had overreacted. She had been groggy from the deep sleep. Maybe she had misread his actions. Kaine would never knowingly take her against her will. But she was going to have to find a way to explain that this was not a favorite moment with him. Her body ached from his rough handling. Her muscles were limp and spent. Why had he treated her so thoughtlessly? She needed a shower and time to get away from him — to think.

She had to get to Luka.

Where had that thought come from?

Given a reprieve since it sounded like Kaine's conversation meant he needed to make different arrangements, she headed for the bath. She was disappointed when the cool, shower water did not wash away her feelings of disgust for Kaine, or guilt of how quickly Luka crept into her thoughts. She'd sought his rescue in the castle when Kaine left her, and his refuge from Kaine now. She began to understand why Luka said it was a matter of time with Kaine. In fact, hadn't Kaine explained about his former girlfriend?

The last one left me because I was too difficult.

The lavender-scented, body wash did not seem to rinse away the lingering stench of the liquor all over her skin. She discovered her body was aching and wounded from Kaine's harsh attention. Her top lip felt puffy in the corner. One of her nipples was inflamed. The upper thigh area and insides ached from his deep thrusts and abrasive touch. She hadn't realized his fingers with the long nails for playing the guitar had been harsh inside her. What the hell had happened to Kaine? She filled with intrepidation again. What if she couldn't get to Luka before Kaine wanted her again, recalling his words of warning in the castle.

I could force you many times and many ways.

How had this happened?

She reeled from her latest experience as Kaine's girlfriend. Holly leaned against the shower wall trying to center her racing thoughts. Kaine, the nefarious rock star had too many secrets. And this was one secret Holly was sure she would never tell the world. But Luka's words came crashing forth warning her again.

He has a violent streak with girlfriends and I wouldn't want to see you crippled in it.

Holly thought Luka to be silly and melodramatic. Was this what Kaine meant when he'd said he was *too hard to handle?* Were Kaine's mercurial mood swings and demanding sexual preferences escalating? Lost in deep thought, Holly didn't notice Kaine entering the bathroom. She heard his deep breathing first, and then she looked up at him. She froze, and studied his face looking for his intentions.

His expression was harsh. "You didn't wait for me." He scolded in a condemning tone.

She cautiously watched his eyes. She didn't want any replays of his temper flaring though she detected something different about him. His lids hung lazy, and his eyes dazed and glassy with more of a faraway look than usual. His beautiful eyes hardened to a leer while they soaked in every curve of her naked body. His tongue crossed his bottom lip and sucked it in as if pondering what to do to her next. Who was this man reacting to her like a disgruntled lover?

Holly's whole body shook nervously. And hoping to avoid any reprisals, she slipped into a robe looping the sash tightly, averting his intense stare. She spoke evenly, placing her back to him.

"I didn't know how long you would be on the phone. There isn't time for me to dress properly for your concert. I want to look my best for you tonight."

She saw Kaine leaned back against the doorway and he

agreed.

"Of course, you're right, counselor. I'll have to hurry if I am to keep up with you."

Cautiously, she watched him reach down to pull off his boot. She exhaled a sigh of relief, thankful he'd accepted her feeble answer but continued to watch his reflection in the mirror as he struggled to get out of his clothes.

With only moments to plan her escape, she waited until his T-shirt was over his head, and then slipped past him darting into the bedroom. The shower started to flow and she exhaled another long breath. She took the ridiculously expensive new dress, from the garment bag and brought it up into view. She called to mind a few hours earlier and the joy in his eyes when he'd picked it out for her. As she dressed in the black-lace Asset lingerie, she had no idea what to think.

What happened?

Hot tears fell from her eyes.

Only one wicked thought branded her mind — how to find Luka.

Chapter Five

BAD LOVE

Holly glanced down at the beautiful, form-fit, black lace dress with the rounded neckline lying on the chair. She swallowed the bile from another wave of disgust, thinking about how brutally Kaine treated her and then how to find Luka. CMT was expecting her for backstage publicity shots. Luka would be there. How differently she felt about him, after this last hour in Hell with Kaine. She looked forward to seeing Luka's warm, blue, angel eyes sparkling at the sight of her.

No, she had to stop thinking of Luka this way. She'd made her choice, and she needed to stick with it as Kaine promised, for good or bad.

She busied herself applying makeup, adding extra foundation around her swollen lip and a little blush to her sunken cheeks, black mascara to her lashes and tinted gloss to her lips. She decided to air dry her long mane and let it fall in ringlets because her shoulders hurt to raise them to style her hair. Quickly flicking back a long lock, she sat on the bed. She was wearing her new black lingerie. Then she slipped on her new two-inch, knee-high, black leather boots.

From the doorway, Kaine whistled, complimenting her stylish fashion of wearing boots and black lingerie.

She stiffened and looked up at him through her eyelashes with unexplained shyness. How could she forgive his drunken lovemaking? If it could be called that. It had been that awful word Luka called it. Fucking. She was sorry to know the difference as she closed her eyes again taking the image of his naked body leaning in the doorway. She opened her eyes to find tears occasionally dropping from his beautiful blue eyes that were begging for her forgiveness.

As if he'd given up, his words broke her heart.

"Go ahead, My Lady. Leave me if you must, I told you I was no good. My love is not healthy or safe. It's not the right love for a loving lady like you. I was hoping I had changed but apparently, all I have is bad love." He closed the distance, and he gently sat beside her and rested his forehead on her shoulder.

He spoke quietly. "It seems I am behaving in ways with you I never thought possible. Here I am again, begging for your forgiveness. I'm not excusing my drunken behavior, but I want to try to explain."

He took another long, labored breath. "There are a lot of things about me I haven't had time to tell you about, and one is ... well, I hope this doesn't compromise you, counselor. You strive to preserve the rules and laws, but Luka had brought drugs ... some dynamite cocaine. It was one of those spontaneous things that happen backstage."

He lifted his chin and looked out of the side of his eyes to study her facial expression. "Please try to understand. I faced a two-hour sound check and three interviews. I have a two and a half hour concert tonight, then a party afterward. I needed a boost. I was buzzed because I haven't done any drugs in four years. Then like a fool, I drank a couple of beers to cut my dry mouth.

"After the sound check, I ran into an old touring mate. We had a few shots of whiskey. Because I've been clean and sober, I don't have a tolerance and it all went straight to my head. When I came back here, I stood by the bedside watching you peacefully sleeping with the moon shadows caressing your beautiful face. My feelings for you were tremendously intense because you were irresistible and gorgeous. I had to be inside you right then.

"You do understand. Today at Asset, you said you wanted me inside you. Only I didn't have a store full of spectators stopping me. I had this incredible hard-on for you...."

He trailed off, took her hand, and held it gently as if she might evaporate any moment.

That was the awful stink!

Whiskey!

Holly was pleased that Kaine confessed to her that his intention had not been what she'd believed. But he needed to understand that he had hurt her in many ways. As forgiveness washed his numerous misdemeanors away, she reached over, and with her free hand lightly stroked his chest, bewildered by her own erratic behavior.

"I'm so bloody sorry, sweetheart. I'm a selfish bastard — again. My only defense, I couldn't think of anything during the sound check but you. I have a million little things to think about and I forgot them all. My only wish was to be here with you." He claimed as his voice faded again.

She sat quiet, because of his words, again, surprising. His heartfelt apology fell on a confused heart. She was about to ask him why they could not act like themselves? Why did they commit these horrible offenses against each other? And point out how painful their love had become.

And, of course, the phone rang.

She didn't move. Neither did he.

They grabbed a hold of each other and tried to block out the loud ring.

"I'm so sorry, My Lady. I'm not handling my new, explosive feelings for you well." He offered as an apology and ventured to kiss her gently on the lips. There was no crushing passion in his kiss as the phone continued to ring, interrupting the backdrop for their crucial reconciliation.

She thought to reassure him by saying. "If you're concerned that I will leave you, I'm not, there are many wonderful things about you Kaine that I'm learning to love. But, I am also finding out about an equally frightening evil twin inside you. And I'm not sure I will — or want to learn to understand him."

He sat up, twisting away from her. His naked back came into full view. Holly reached over to touch him but stopped. Eight, deep, bloody nail marks were carved into the length of his flesh. She had literally torn up his back. The welts were thick and already caked with dried blood. A profound disgust swept over her as she moved closer to him, she saw the scarred wounds and recollected their first shower together and his puzzling words.

Too ugly to talk about while I'm so happy.

Someone had beat him, hurt him badly, hated him and not once.

Her words tumbled out as quickly.

"Oh, my Precious One."

She pleaded softly.

"Please forgive me."

As her fingertips delicately touched, his back where she'd left her marks.

From inside his throat, his muffled words fell quickly.

"Forgive you? I hurt you. I have done something unforgivable to you. When I got into the shower, the hot water instantly burned my back. I couldn't understand what the hell happened?" Kaine turned around to face her. He relaxed, stretching out his nude body on his side behind her and propped his head up on his palm.

"I looked into the mirror to see what was causing me the excruciating pain and I discovered the gashes. I'm not stupid, My Lady, and know the difference between light scratches left during passionate moments and a terrified woman struggling for freedom from my forcefulness. I felt fucking awful Holly. I can't imagine what you were thinking. I've been in there wondering how to face you.

"You're not a bimbo, hanging around backstage to fuck me. You're My Lady, my woman, my girlfriend. I've promised never to hurt you, to take care of you, and provide for you. Not terrify you."

And he trailed off, "...sorry, I hurt you."

Kaine swiftly reached out and gently pulled her down into his arms. He kissed her lovingly, tenderly, showing her his deep sorrow for hurting her, hoping to convince her, he would not bring pain to her again.

Was Holly going to interrupt this moment of reunion and explain to Kaine that he had terrified her to the point she'd planned to leave him and run to Luka?

Chapter Six

HIT ME WITH YOUR BEST SHOT

How long would their peace treaty last? Would she ever have the secret key to keeping Kaine happy? He was a man trapped in an impossible world, eager to shed his rock star armor with her. He seemingly wanted to become a man, a gentle man, unassuming, kind, and patient. She recollected Kaine's warning at the castle.

Some can't cut my lifestyle, and I hope you love me enough to get through the fucked times because I love you.

Well, this was the second of the fucked times. She wondered if her budding love for the sweet and sensitive man was strong enough to endure the mighty Kaine, a drug, and booze-fueled rock star.

Dizzy from the evening's events, a harsh, intrusive knock crashed against the door jarring her from her analysis.

"Kaine? Now! Kaine! Security is ready. The fucking car is waiting! We bloody well have to go, now!" Luka's voice demanded as his fist punctuated every three or four words on the trembling hotel door.

Luka's arrival meant there would be no putting him off this time.

"Fuck! Holly, we forgot Wembley!" Kaine said, leaping up, his eyes lit with surprise.

"Just a minute," Kaine yelled as if no bad blood ran between him and Luka.

Theirs was a curious relationship but she wondered why Luka brought the cocaine backstage and shared it with Kaine? That must mean they were playing brothers again. Why would Luka interfere with Kaine's sobriety? Holly tossed her hair back, confused by Kaine's friendly response to Luka. She watched him sprint into the bathroom like a bad boy caught and had to appease the disgruntled schoolmaster. It wasn't hard to see which one was in control of the situation.

To straighten her back she stood and hooked her black, lace bra, and slipped into her dress. It had purple satin buttons to match the piping, and they were spaced from the collar to the hem. While she tediously pushed each button into its matching hole, Kaine's voice flowed from the bathroom.

"Answer the door counselor. Tell Luka I'll be out starightaway."

Too embarrassed to face Luka, she braced herself for the next squall by smoothing her hair with her fingers and tried to block out Luka's persistent pounding.

The last few buttons were left undone around her bodice as she swung past the beverage cart, picked up a beer with one hand and a slice of lime in the other. She took a long swig and bit down on the lime as she opened the door.

She grabbed a breath.

Luka....

There he was leaning in the doorway.

He was breathtaking, though, his expression was tight and harsh, prepared for a fight. His facial muscles instantly softened at the sight of her. The Luka she knew reappeared, his angel eyes brightened, clearly happy to see her. It was good to see him too.

Maybe too good.

Her sense of relief faded fast as his words pierced her.

His beautiful face took on a cold, menacing facade.

"What's the fucker done to you?" He demanded as his fingertip traced the corner of her swollen lip.

"Ow..." slipped out. She'd forgotten Kaine's drug propelled kisses had left her lip both cut and puffy.

"Nothing, everything's fine." She managed in as positive a tone as possible.

Luka did not believe her. He took a step closer and taking his usual liberty, pressed his firm body against hers and pulled her into his arms. His warm, moist lips reverently brushed her cheek. He held her tight as if afraid to let her go.

He was familiar, felt good, better than good like she'd come home. She needed to move away from Luka and when she prepared to take a step he spoke into her hair, near her ear.

"Are you sure you don't want me to take care of him? I can ... call in a favor."

She looked at Luka positive the astonishment flashed over her face. How could he suggest such a thing?

"Okay Babe, relax. Let me hold you. I won't let anything like this happen to you again," he bellowed with a threatening tone in his voice that told Holly to calm him down immediately.

She straightened her back and leaned to the right to peer into his eyes packed with anger. Stormy, blue eyes that said he was dead serious. Uncomfortable with Luka's insinuation about *taking care of him,* and afraid of what that would mean, she wondered how powerful Luka was? Then again, she wasn't sure she wanted to know.

Luka's strong arm circled her waist and drew her in again, and pressed her against his full body as he hugged her with relief. He spoke into her ear. "I won't let that bastard ever hurt you again."

Luka had been right all along, but that didn't stop Holly from trying to squirm out of his claustrophobic embrace. Luka's promise meant to soothe her only caused her greater distress. He held on to her tenaciously and all she could do was give in, relaxing against his chest, draped in a crisp, white shirt under a rough, black-leather tailored jacket. He pressed his 501 Levi, clad leg between hers. Luka was doing it again, swallowing her whole, as he hugged her tightly.

She pulled back again and stared into his eyes, his blue, angel eyes to-die-for, and found him too beautiful with his golden hair, damp, framing his angelic face. She allowed a negligible sigh to escape because he was overpowering.

Luka winked and then kissed her cheek meaningful. He pushed his way past her yelling out, "You fucker. How could you hurt her like that?" Luka demanded answers and vanishing into the bedroom with Kaine.

Holly swelled with an immediate panic as loud, muffled voices poured from the doorway, then a scuffle, like hard objects crashing into something harder. She raced to the doorway. Her heart pounded with dread and her jaw dropped open. She found Kaine pinned against the wall, Luka pressing his hands around Kaine's throat. Kaine's face was bright red, the veins in his forehead popping out. Yet Luka would not back away. Kaine was gasping for breath as Holly sprinted to pull Luka from Kaine. But not before Kaine punched Luka hard, in the ribs, forcing Luka to release his grip.

Luka grabbed his side, cursed and backed away and yelled.

"We're not finished, you bastard!"

Kaine sputtered, attempting to catch his breath, swallowing large amounts of air while trying to speak.

"Tell 'em. Tell him Holly."

But Luka returned inches from Kaine.

Holly dared to slip between the two of them, facing Luka.

Luka's eyes were bulging and flashing with varying degrees of anger. He seemed to be fighting with himself if it was right to pull back.

She saw it was a struggle for him and then he finally backed off and stopped.

His eyes narrowed to slits, telling Kaine, he'd meant what he'd said. They were not finished.

Holly wondered for a moment how high on cocaine Luka was. Was that part of the cause for this assault on Kaine? This world moved too fast. She hadn't time to evaluate Kaine's return from the sound check or to referee a fistfight.

Holly lifted a mineral water from the nightstand and handed it to Kaine. She struggled for the words that upset her because they were lies.

"Luka, truly, I'm all right. We got a little carried away."

Luka looked at her searching for the truth.

She saw he was trying to decide if he should believe her.

"Really...." she repeated in her most reassuring tone, sorry to lie to him. His instincts were right on and he deserved better.

Luka straightened his spine while adjusting his jacket. His eyes returned to the deep blue color she loved. But his facial expression hadn't changed. He took a single step backward, turned and his voice followed his heels demanding.

"Get him ready ... straightaway ... we're late."

Chapter Seven

COCAINE

Holly couldn't let go of the blaze of sensual thoughts as she walked hand-in-hand with Kaine down the corridor.

They were flanked by three, big, brawny, security men on each side of them. So much for a private moment. The sound check and fist fight were already forgotten because they were on the move again. No time to think, to wonder or analyze anything.

Kaine threw a glance to Luka and mentioned casually.

"More threats?"

"Nothing unusual." Luka's face didn't flinch, his tone of voice said they were mates again.

Holly dropped her chin to her chest. They were talking about death threats and Kaine had been right, she had no idea what she had gotten herself into by loving him.

Everyone squeezed into the tiny elevator car. Behind her was the labored breathing of stuffed sinuses from one bodyguard. Otherwise, the ride down was subdued, if sandwiched between Kaine and Luka could ever be described as subdued.

Neither Luka or Kaine prepared Holly for when the doors opened. There surrounding the doorway, five feet deep, was Fleet Street, the paparazzi, and seemingly every rock video and print reporter available. This was far worse than the court steps outside the Collins murder trial.

The unimaginable started.

The crowd pushed and clawed its way forward, with one focus, to get closer to Kaine. Holly took a step backward, watching the no nonsense security men, unmercifully hit and kick a clear pathway in front of Kaine. Her anxiety quickly rose, especially when Kaine's hand became more and more slippery as the sweat oozed from her palms until he finally slipped from her grasp and the manic crowd instantly swallowed him.

Holly was left to the mercy of the riotous mob of fans and media. Loud screams and more deafening yells burst near her ears while greedy, disrespectful hands pawed at her body. Her hair was pulled in all four directions at once. The knot in her stomach burned with panic as the media's camera's bombarded her with bright strobe lights, blinding her. Brash voices were hurling vulgar questions, demanding she reveal her secrets because she was a secret no more. The press knew who she was.

"How did you meet Kaine?"

"Where are you from?"

"Are you the Holly Hill from the Collins murder trial?"

It was then she was asked the question that sent raging fear through her body.

"Are you fucking Luka Hunter?"

She turned around and no one in the sea of faces gave themselves away. She frantically pushed and shoved with more conviction.

She needed to get to Kaine.

Where in the hell are you, Kaine?

She wailed in the dark halls of her frightened mind.

Trapped in a crowd that resembled a living, breathing, creature lobbing its way across the quaint foyer, she was caught between the press, the hangers-on, and fanatic fans. Her terror grew quickly, worried if she would find Kaine before she was hurt or worse, trampled. There was another round of squeals of delight ahead. More fans had caught sight of Kaine. She struggled and shoved the bodies blocking her path, hoping to reach the safety of the waiting car. But no matter how hard she tried, she could not break free of the moving spectacle.

The crowd launched Holly outside the hotel door, like birthing a baby. Holly spotted the hood of the white Bentley through the hovering crowd. Not a moment too soon, a firm hand grasped her upper arm. She welcomed the familiar arm circling her waist, reeling her in close, oh so close.

Luka pulled her body to him and then securely into his arms. His eyes said something his lips didn't dare to speak. His eyes sparkled and seemed to say he welcomed the frenzied crowd crushing their bodies together. He smiled as he rubbed her breasts pressed flat against his chest, and placed her hips flush against his. It wasn't her imagination. Luka rubbed against her with sensual overtones. She may be with Kaine, but Luka, what the hell was she going to do about Luka?

An overzealous fan pulled on her hair and Luka backhanded him. True to his word, he didn't want anyone to hurt her. Luka wrapped his arm around her tight to keep her beside him. It was then she realized what the hard lump was that nudged her shoulder. This was not her imagination either. Luka was carrying a gun, so much for the romantic fairy tale. This was the darker side of the music business.

Luka covered her head with his jacket. He shielded her with his tall, muscular body and ushered her through the crushing crowd to safety in the back seat of the Bentley. Luka slammed the door shut, locking it quickly. He sat back beside her, sandwiching her tightly between him and Kaine. Settled in, Luka dropped his hand to rest it comfortably on her thigh in plain view of Kaine. The chauffeur cautiously honked the horn to clear a path as he inched the car through the massive mob.

"Haven't seen one of these crowds in years?" Luka commented. "You see Kaine. You're as popular as ever. The four years in seclusion have only heightened the mystique about you."

A sea of anonymous faces pressed their fleshly features against the Bentley's smoked glass windows displaying a most grotesque picture. The wailing sounds of the fans hands and fists pounded on the roof of the car and shot constant waves of alarm through Holly. It was then Kaine's comforting hand slipped around her quivering shoulder and pulled her into his trustworthy embrace.

Luka's hand dropped onto the seat with a thud.

"It's okay, Holly. We're safe." Kaine reassured to comfort her while nuzzling into her hair and then kissed her ear.

She acknowledged his words by squeezing his arm, but she was not sure she was convinced.

Blocks away from the hysterical crowd, Holly breathed a bit better.

Kaine started complaining to Luka and yelled. "What the fuck did you think you were doing Hunter? You left Holly back there in that fucking insane crowd! Why the fuck didn't we leave by an alternate route? She might have been seriously injured!"

"Hell of a time to start worrying about her safety." Luka shot back, his voice dripping with coldness.

They all understood what he meant.

She fought the impulse to touch her puffy lip. "I'm all right." Holly threw in flatly. She was forever reassuring these men of her well-being.

"Where is security?" Kaine demanded.

"I am not bloody responsible. Talk to your new tour manager. He's the tosser." Luka claimed and then shot Kaine a dirty look.

Kaine sat back fuming, rubbing his throat. "Throw me a mineral water," he demanded of Luka.

"Here, use this instead. Your throat will be numb enough to perform."

"Thank you, Doctor Luka, for your prognosis," Kaine shot back venomously. "My throat fucking hurts from your stupid stunt in my bedroom."

"Stop wanking. It wouldn't have happened if you'd bloody

well listened to me. I warned you about her." Luka lambasted Kaine as he leaned over Holly an inch from Kaine's face.

She'd had enough. They were leaning over her, face-to-face.

"Luka ... Kaine... ." Holly shouted, pushing the two apart before another fight broke out. And in the confines of the Bentley, with two bodyguards, there simply wasn't enough room for them to have another go around with the Testosterone Twins.

Luka leaned back beside her, his face red with fury. He pulled a small glass vial from his pocket. He flung it to Kaine, who caught it, midair.

Kaine sat quiet, holding the bottle.

"Well?" Luka challenged, looking at Kaine from the sides of his eyes.

Kaine hesitated. He opened the bottle and held the tiny spoon attached. He filled one side of his nose with sparkling crystals, inhaled, and repeated the process on the other side. When he consumed enough, he quietly sat back, ran his fingers through his hair, curled his index finger, and pinched his nose with his thumb. But he wouldn't look at her.

Luka reached over for the vial, but she intercepted it. She didn't want Kaine so embarrassed by his drug use that he wouldn't even look at her. She wanted to defuse the situation, fast. She also selfishly hoped this drug might make her forget the quarrels between Luka and Kaine.

Drugs — another new one for her, as she mimicked Kaine's movements, filling the spoon generously and then inhaled deeply.

Kaine watched her curiously.

"Breaking the law counselor?"

"Wouldn't be the first time." She teased and then smiled.

He didn't smile back at her. His eyes grew more serious, and he reached out for the vial.

She stopped him. Funny he would care. Perhaps he wanted more. But the protection in his eyes, told her, he wasn't certain he wanted her doing drugs. That was something she'd never considered. In the jaded world he lived in, she figured it was perfectly normal to do cocaine on the way to concerts, even if she was a lady, one test away from her license to practice law. As she slipped more into the ways of the outlaws of her time, she wondered what would come next.

Holly couldn't think anymore. The crystal powder was blasting her sinuses, firing potent bolts of energy throughout her tired, battered body. The power and vitality were instant. Her discomfort from the bruising crowd and Kaine's rough handling vanished. Everything was replaced with a vibrant alertness that surpassed euphoria.

Luka did the other side of her nose, to even the freeze, as he quaintly called it. She sat back energized in Kaine's loving arms. All the grueling trials of the afternoon and evening melting away and she eagerly anticipated the second performance of the world-class act, *Hurrikaine*.

Holly arrived at Wembley Arena escorted by the two handsomest men in the universe.

Everything was different.

Kaine's life did change drastically — every few hours. It was all she could do to keep up with the exhaustive pace. There was precious little time to reflect on anything long enough to come to a rational conclusion because it was time to change again. She latched on to Kaine's hand as he reached into the car for her.

It was showtime. Kaine had arrived.

Holly stepped into a ready-made spotlight used to highlight Kaine's triumphant entrance. Pride washed over her as she stood beside him in the glare of the public eye. She'd become the visiting rock princess, not Holly Hill from the Collins murder trial.

The strong camera lights were blinding, but she saw that the dazzling effects did not impress Kaine. She admired how well adjusted he was with his jaded, but glamorous rock star life. But for him, fame had come gradually, over many years, and he'd been educated in what to do, what to expect. But she was mesmerized, dropped into this mysterious atmosphere, and suddenly she appreciated his guidance.

They trailed Luka, who cleared the path and watched all directions for Kaine's safety. She followed the two men whose lives depended so much on each other. They hurried through the human security chain, then the backstage entrance. They passed more security and climbed the stairs meant only for the gold laminated elite. Heavy security blocked the doorway. They were finally safe in the dressing room.

Luka snapped a gold *Hurrikaine,* all access backstage pass on to Holly's dress. Holly's numbered thirty-six, Kaine's was number two, Luka's number one.

That said it all.

Holly noticed the setup was the same as the earlier concert. Along one wall, the buffet table, draped with white linen, was topped with a large selection of snacks. To the left was a full bar. She hadn't any appetite, but her mouth was parched. She picked up a beer and added a slice of lime. She chugged it dry and grabbed another. The only thing different, she arrived with Kaine, not merely anticipating meeting him for the first time. How much had changed in three days!

Luka called her over to where Kaine stood. Photos were taken with Kaine for CMT's documentary on the *Hurrikaine* tour. Interviews started and when asked candidly to share her thoughts about the contest she confidently stated.

"Winning has changed my life." She smiled graciously and then squeezed Kaine's hand meaningfully.

Holly wandered about in the large dressing room admiring the 50s jukebox playing blues and a pool table used by two stylishly dressed men. She was buzzing with energy, filled with wonderful feelings of well-being. With her obligations of the moment satisfied, she scanned the room.

It was then, over by the bar, a lean, expensively dressed, blonde beauty entered the room and headed straight for Luka. The beautiful woman threw her arms around his neck, firing words at him in broken English, perhaps a German accent. Then she kissed Luka as if they shared a long history. That was acceptable, what Holly didn't like was Luka returning the kiss. No one in the dressing room seemed to care the least bit or paid any interest in Luka with the woman. Yet they captured Holly's full attention. Holly fought closing her eyes to remember how wonderful it felt to have Luka hold her tight in his arms. She wanted to look away, but she couldn't.

Luka walked the woman up against the wall.

Must be his technique.

He pressed the woman with his body, but Holly pictured his body on hers. How perfectly she'd fit with Luka's. She sighed, missing the times when she had been the focus of his attention, only a few hours earlier. How fast time flew.

Luka molded the length of him into the woman's long curved body. His long hair shimmered as it cascaded to the side, blocking the kiss. She didn't like how glad he'd been to see her, but it was as it should be.

After a few more moments watching the intimate display, Holly couldn't take any more of his kissing the woman because thoughts were crowding her mind. How long did he intend to kiss the woman?

Disgusted, she turned and walked away. She didn't like the fact that Luka's demonstration of affection for another woman was getting under her skin. Luka wasn't hers. Yet something inside her registered a grave loss.

Holly grabbed another beer, drained it, and wished she could have another hit of the white, miracle powder. She noticed the other corner of the enormous room was bleak and nondescript. That was until her eyes settled on long, flaming red hair. Beneath, there were harsh green eyes staring back at her. They were glaring with disgust under fringed bangs. The bright green eyes bragged how much they loathed Holly. The woman's stare was intense forcing Holly to break away. Who was this obnoxious woman with the venom in her eyes?

Holly searched her memory for a red-haired bimbo. Back to the hotel? No. The castle? No. The video shoot? No. Then where?

All Holly knew was that from across the room, she was picking up the deadliest vibes.

What had Holly done?

Chapter Eight

TAINTED LOVE

olly averted the redheads' vicious glare. No matter where Holly moved, the woman's stare followed her like the eyes of a picture on a wall. The woman may have been quite pretty, once. Her pale face was painted gothic with heavy makeup. She'd stuffed her well-endowed breasts into a black bustier. Her long, willowy legs were clad in black Spandex, but it only accentuated her whorish demeanor. Her single asset was long, beautiful red hair that spilled down over her pumped up breasts.

The vicious woman skirted the outer edges of the dressing room, heading straight for her, while her green eyes darted from Kaine, then to Holly.

Holly tried to avoid all eye contact, but the woman was closing the distance between them. The strange woman moved in close and her inexpensive perfume swamped Holly's senses as the woman towered above her in spiked heels.

There was nowhere else to look except into the redheads hate filled eyes. There she found a full measure of loathing meant for anyone who threatened her. Holly wasn't certain what to do?

In a thick, coarse British accent, the red-haired woman shared to belittle Holly.

"I've seen Kaine with tarts like you, a thousand times. He'll use you for whatever he wants and after a few days, be tired of fucking you. Then he will come back to me, he always does! So, fuck off ... you cow!"

Holly's eyebrows must have pushed up her forehead. The horrid woman's evil revelation made Holly take a full step backward, and she didn't speak right away. She was processing the outburst. What did she mean? *Go back to her.* Who the hell was this redheaded bitch?

Holly looked her in the eyes and countered loudly. "We'll see about that honey!"

She thought to add profanity, but her thoughts were temporarily interrupted when Ian, the bands keyboard player, made a late entrance.

Ian didn't look much different from the Hard Rock video shoot. His attractive, shaggy, blond hair, dripped lazily about his shoulders. He revealed a sunny billboard smile, which he shared with her.

Ian's head swiftly turned, glared at her, and demanded.

"Fuck off bitch...."

The redhead drew in her claws and backed off. She walked away launching one nasty look after the other at Holly every few feet.

"That fuckin' Sarah thinks she owns Kaine. Don't let her upset you. Rah, as we call her, is Kaine's personal assistant. All business on his part, I assure you. But she's dim and doesn't seem to get it through her thick head, Kaine ain't interested." Ian insisted and paused.

He added, flicking his incredible sun-streaked hair out of his eyes. "Why should he? He has a classy girlfriend like you now." He flashed an accepting smile.

Ian stepped closer to Holly. "It will get amazingly rough around Kaine. Don't fool yourself and think you can handle it and take on Rah. She doesn't play fair when it comes to Kaine. She's messed up a few women over the years. If Rah gives you any trouble, find me quickly and I'll take care of her." He glanced around, "I'm late. Need to see what's happening. Talk later ... Holly isn't it?"

"Yes," she answered, "Holly Hill. It has been nice and interesting meeting you?" She said in a tone of asking who he was.

"Ian. Ah, my dog has better manners, Ian Montgomery, at your service. Holler if you need me."

"I will ... Ian." She released a chuckle, smiled generously at her new friend, and then looked over to find Kaine smiling charitably at Ian, who joined him. Soon they were laughing and Kaine leaned against a stack of equipment, comfortable with himself. He worked the room, giving interviews and schmoozing with the same ease in the boutique. He was the perfect rock star.

She watched him catch a glimpse of her and he flashed his bracketed dimples for her. A cold rush, emanated from Sarah, as she stood inches from Kaine as if to mark her territory.

It was then a young, harried man rushed into the dressing room.

"When you're ready," he yelled.

Luka led the parade with the blonde-haired woman. The

band's roadies and CMT's film crew followed the hangers-on after the man. All that remained were the band and their women, Kaine, Holly, and Sarah along with a legion of security men.

Kaine sensing the rooms chill and spun around. He instantly pinned the source.

"Rah, go to Luka, straightaway!" He shouted at her in a harsh tone.

Sarah didn't move.

Kaine shot Sarah a glaring look. "I said go!"

Kaine's voice was loud and furious as he blurted the words between clenched teeth.

Sarah's eyes were full of deadly venom as she viciously glanced at Holly. She nonchalantly sauntered out of the room, but not before, she took the chance to pass inches from Holly. Sarah made sure Kaine couldn't see or hear her and threatened.

"You're fucking history ... bitch!" Then she vanished into the corridor.

Before Holly had a clear thought, Kaine's scent surrounded her.

"You, My Lady Love, are with me," Kaine reassured, his words meant to encourage her.

She let Kaine take her hand gently and squeezed his in return. Kaine Walker, the man of the hour, led her out of the hideaway flanked by security, the band, their companions, with the CMT cameras whirling. Holly followed Kaine down the stairs, across the lounge area to behind the stage. He twirled around and swept her into his arms.

"I have to get away for a few minutes to collect my thoughts."

She smiled, remembering his ritual. She lightly brushed her lips against his and confessed.

"You're the most wonderful man in the world Kaine Walker, and I do love you."

He made a moist path to her ear where he whispered, "I love you too, and tonight I sing for you."

Chapter Nine

STRANGELOVE

Holly followed Kaine behind the human security chain as far as a non-performer could. Next came the special squeeze of her hand before Kaine vanished like a phantom into the thick, gray smoke. She caught a glimpse of Ian a few feet from her, vigorously hugging a statuesque, elegantly dressed woman. Coincidentally, the same woman Kaine walked away with at the castle. She'd had a strange foreign name. The lady wore a black, tailored Asset suit over a sheer, white-laced blouse. The high fashioned look flattered her waif-model frame and Ian seemed ecstatic to bathe in her good luck kisses. The longing in his eyes reflected his reluctance to leave her, but he hugged her lovingly, whirled around, and vanished into the hungry smoke.

A firm, familiar hand circled her waist. She expected to find Luka. He didn't disappoint her. She had wondered how long it would take him to get back to her. She bristled, remembering the beautiful, blonde model in his arms earlier. She smelled the woman's pricey perfume that hung like a dismal cloud about Luka. Green-eyed jealousy stabbed at her as she noticed the smudges of ruby lipstick where he'd tried to wipe them off his skin.

Why did she care? And while on the subject, why did she respond like that damn moth to the flame every time Luka touched her? Because there was that helpless feeling, again, of knowing, she was his puppet and he held the invisible strings, surely to control her.

"Everything all right?" He whispered thickly.

No, nothing was all right.

She picked up the edge of his scarf and placed the tip in her mouth to dampen it. She attempted to wipe the lip imprint off his chin.

"I'm glad to see you haven't forgotten me," he whispered as a satisfied smile curled his lips, and he pulled her closer, threatening to kiss her.

Holly backed away because she'd forgiven Kaine, his rough treatment and was devoted to him.

"No? Not yet?" Luka teased.

He stopped a breath away from her lips, so close the heat of his breath and his fresh scent surrounded her.

"No, I'm not going to kiss you," he laughed, threw his head back cockily and smiled his sexy boyish smile.

"Though I can see you need my kisses badly. But I'm going to let you miss me a bit longer."

"Damn you, Luka Hunter!" She admonished as she tried to bolt from his locked embrace. His cocky attitude infuriated her.

His kisses. Indeed!

"I said I wouldn't kiss you. I didn't say I'm ready to let you out of my arms. I rather like you jealous," he chuckled and continued. "Babe, the blonde's nothing to me, business, a one-off. Don't worry about her. Look, I have someone over here Kaine wants you to meet." Luka dropped his arms and Holly reluctantly allowed him to take her hand. He pulled her toward the beautiful creature Ian had left standing alone.

But all that was circling Holly's mind was Luka.

Jealous?

One off?

What did that mean?

Who the hell did Luka think he was? Holly fought a childish urge to stomp on Luka's foot, for teasing her as he did.

She lifted an indignant eyebrow.

"Why I'd love to meet Kaine's friend." She was eager to meet a lady on the tour. Maybe she had answers.

"Smashing. I knew I could count on you. Since you're Kaine's girlfriend — *for now*! I think you're ready to meet the family."

She'd heard him. *For now.*

It took Luka a second to break her cool composure. He seemed to enjoy her frustration, holding her tightly against him, closer than necessary. He smiled with satisfaction as he walked her up to the lady.

"Holly, this lady is Solange Beauvais, Ian's *longtime* girlfriend."

"Solange, Kaine's *new* girlfriend, Holly Hill. She's been wasting her time with him. I've been trying to convince her to fall in love with me. Unfortunately, she has a stubborn mind of her own and I can't seem to change it."

"Sounds like she has good sense," the woman said with a

crisp French accent.

Holly instantly liked her.

Solange's face filled with a warm, friendly smile, yet she stared at Holly with sheer amazement growing steadily in her eyes. The resemblance to Luka's former lover had struck again.

"Some bloody help you're going to be," Luka criticized lightheartedly and laughed. "Kaine asked if you would please show Holly where to sit while the band plays? I have the usual last-minute business."

"Wee, of course. Let me find Emily and tell her where to meet after the concert. I'll be about fifteen minutes," she offered, speaking to Holly to set her at ease. Solange turned to vanish into the gray-white smoke that drenched the entire backstage area.

Holly couldn't see a foot in front of her.

Luka didn't waste a moment. He pulled her into a curtained section, away and out-of-sight. He poured two, fat lines of cocaine on the top of black equipment stenciled with twelve-inch white letters that spelled out *Hurrikaine* and handed her a long thin glass cylinder.

"Quickly, you bloody will love this batch."

Holly leaned in to fill first one nostril, then the other. The jet-propelled drug instantly exploded in her head. She closed her eyes, enjoying the rush, leaning onto Luka as his warm, familiar arms circled her. She settled in for the seductive drug rush. She didn't even notice his soft cheek brush against hers. She didn't mind the lightness of his sweet, moist lips brushing her cheek, or his words in her ear until he tried to persuade her again.

"Come with me before it's too late."

Holly turned around in his arms to move away.

Luka was faster. His lips found hers, exactly when the cocaine exploded in her head he kissed her again, and again, and again. Her sense of inhibition was melting. Her lips hungrily responded to him. Luka was doing it, emptying her mind, then demanding her body. She fell helpless under his command.

And so it was as her spirit became lost in his soul-stealing kiss. A kiss so powerful, she couldn't remember her original complaint.

Luka broke the kiss, spoke faintly, and pleaded into her ear.

"Come with me before it's too late."

Holly quickly pulled away. "You have to stop this. I can't fight you."

"That's all I need to hear. It's only a matter of time." Luka poured two more lines.

She was shaking her head no.

He insisted. "Quickly, before someone comes."

The crystal powder surged through her veins, recharging her, knocking her off balance. She fell into Luka's broad chest. His strong arms came to her rescue, wrapping tightly around her. "I can't..." She tried to say, but the drug was potent and the rush rendered her mute.

Her eyes must sparkle too because as she looked up to Luka, he sparkled. He was beautiful — fucking beautiful. She watched his tongue dart out to polish his lips. His glistening mouth moved toward her. Holly slid her hands up his soft, leather jacket, stepping closer to him as natural as taking a breath. And oh, those succulent, rosy lips of his, how they begged her to kiss them, again, and again.

Luka tilted his head. His mouth soft and warm, pressed carefully, not to hurt her swollen lip. Luka was doing it again, making her forget who she was, or how he was seducing her. Nothing in the world seemed to matter, except the burning inside that wanted him. The burn compelled her to give in and relax her hips on him. His hand twisted in her hair as his other hand dropped to the small of her back, pressing her against the swell in his pants.

Luka wanted her.

Good.

Luka kissed her breath away, dancing a slow lover's waltz with her, his lips seared to hers, no beginning, and no end. Luka released her and pressed her head against his chest until his breath ran even.

What would she call this scorching, sense of burning she shared with Luka? Was it drug-fueled lust? Suddenly, the horrible flooding of shame forced its way into her head. It carried one word.

Kaine.

There is a limit.

She swiftly pushed away from Luka, but apparently not quick enough. The heat of guilt and humiliation already engulfed her face, and then her body. Lastly, the flash of disgrace arrived to lash at her, because of her lusty attention to Luka. She hated drowning in the suffocating betrayal. Her hands rolled into tiny balls. She placed them on Luka's chest to push him away.

But Luka thought differently. His tight embrace prevented

her escape.

A cold, backstage draft whirled up between her legs and she squeezed her thighs together to stop the wetness made by Luka. Her shame doubled as hot burning tears assaulted her eyes. Kaine's words echoed in her head. *What kind of woman are you?* She pressed on Luka's chest hard, harder still. But Luka squeezed her tightly forcing her to stop.

"Shhh...."

He whispered.

"You have nothing to be ashamed of because you showed me how I make you feel. I don't think less of you. In fact, I would say, my every thought will be of you." He'd asserted smiling, twisting that sexy grin of his around his lips.

"Shut up Luka!" she sassed.

"Acting like this isn't right. Moments ago, you introduced me as his girlfriend. I ... I can't be with you." She argued realizing she couldn't even say Kaine's name.

"I've got news. You already have. You were incredibly passionate and...."

She cut him off because she couldn't listen to him say the betraying words. "Damn you! You've pumped me full of cocaine and seduced me, Luka. How could you?"

"You do realize, I could have shown you a taste of what real loving is all about, Babe. Instead, I've held back. I could have just as easily thrown you to the floor and fucked your brains out and don't think you would have stopped me. But I care for you and because of that, I have followed your lead. Even now, your body isn't bloody well finished with me. You and I have unfinished business."

Holly was shocked by his words, his truth.

His hand quickly moved up under her short dress to the wetness between her legs. He looked at her, locked onto her eyes as he touched her there, daring her to stop him. He didn't say a word. The proof was there, glistening on his hand when he brought it up into view.

He'd shocked her again.

Hoping for a breath that would give her the time for a retort, she shook her head and challenged him.

"How can you be certain that isn't for Kaine?"

"I doubt it. It doesn't take much coaxing from me to take your mind off him. I intend to win your heart soon and then your soul." And to prove his intent, his mouth came crashing down hard on hers as she squirmed in his tight embrace.

But Luka was demanding.

"I can't!" She claimed, disputing his words, weakened a bit and then broke away. Frustrated she stepped back on her heels and looked away from Luka.

He let go of her.

No, she couldn't look at him. He was right. A part of her did belong to him. She'd proven it again to Luka and to herself. He would never let her stay with Kaine. It was as he said, just a matter of time.

Luka cupped her chin, pulling her face inches from his.

How much she wanted to love him, and how much she wanted to push him away. She was half in love with him, half in hate with him. She looked up at him and sighed, exhaling a defeated breath.

"Holly, don't look at me with those eyes. I see you're in an impossible position. But please don't deny what you're feeling. You're too bloody hard on yourself. You're a beautiful, loving woman. Don't stop what you feel for me."

"I can't do this Luka. I've gone from you to Kaine, then back to you, then back to Kaine again, and now. This is Hell! I am beginning to feel like a whore ... and I can't take anymore."

It was true, each round with these two virile men, the stakes were raised. She didn't know if she had the required strength to endure until the last round of this contest. One traitorous tear spilled down her cheek.

Luka's lips were there to catch it with a soft kiss. "Stop this madness," he demanded. "Come with me before it's too late."

Holly stared at Luka, placing a stray strand of golden threads behind his tiny ear.

Luka asked with an edge of urgency. "Stay with me?"

"No." She refused in a firm tone, hoping he would accept her final word.

Luka poured another line, thinner this time. "I haven't time to argue. I'm expected straightaway. You need to meet up with Solange." Then he laid out two more lines to fill both sides of her nose.

Her heart pounded, screaming to break through her chest. She looked up at Luka.

He opened his arms, and she went to him.

He embraced her and made no move on her.

"Is this how I'm supposed to feel?" she asked in a weak voice.

"How is that?"

"Like if I let go of you, I'll float away?"

He chuckled and explained, "It means this is a superb blow. Hold onto me until you're in control."

It hadn't been two seconds before she became aware of his body. It was horrible, wanting him and fighting the guilt because she did. Yet, the twisting guilt did not cool her appetite for the sexy Luka Hunter. The urge to step away from Luka evaporated, and she moved her lips near his neck, nuzzling into him, as he held her like a familiar lover. She wondered if she should kiss him the way she wanted to because no one would see and Luka counted on this drug to render her vulnerable.

He waited for her.

His pink tipped tongue darted out before he gave in to her.

"Okay, one kiss, and then you have to go...."

He came in close to her lips, the warmth of his breath blew softly. He pressed her lips, waiting for her to open her mouth to let him consume her. He pulled her so close nothing could come between them. He entered slowly and then kissed her deeply, lovingly, a sensual kiss, confirming he still had a better than even chance of having her for himself. Especially if she would come to him this willing after the world believed known, she was Kaine's girlfriend. His kiss told her she was not going to stay Kaine Walker's girlfriend for long.

Her kiss told him she agreed. It was just a matter of time.

Lost in the misty darkness, Holly forgot everyone and everything. There were only Luka and his incredible soul-destroying kiss. She floated, missing in time. Holly finally pulled away from the searing kiss as the initial rush of the drug started to subside. She gazed, glassy-eyed up at her handsome angel.

"It's okay." He quietly revealed to calm her. "I had to see for myself. Do whatever your conscience dictates. I'm not far away."

He let go of her and took hold of her hands from around his neck, brought them together in front of him and squeezed.

"I only want to bring you happiness."

"Luka, I'm not sure anymore what will make me happy."

She looked up into his beautiful blue eyes, stepped back, turned, and walked into the mist. He followed and placed his hand gently on her shoulder for encouragement. She couldn't face him. She couldn't look into his angel eyes and see the ache she'd left there. She couldn't touch his warm skin again. If she did, she was afraid she wouldn't fight these powerful inner urges. She wasn't strong enough to fight herself and him.

Holly kept walking, one foot in front of the other, as fast as she could. Her heart ached, repeatedly stabbed from the raging war between her mind, body, heart, and soul. She walked quicker. She was running away from Luka into the mist. She shared a strange love with Luka and his hold on her was growing stronger every time she was near him. If she didn't realize it before, she did now.

Stay away from Luka Hunter!

Stay far, far away.

Chapter Ten

STRANGER THAN FICTION

Those hot, sensuous kisses with Luka could have cost her Kaine. Where was her usual sense of good judgment? Luka caught up to her, took hold of her wrist, and pressed a small, glass vial into the palm of her hand. He brushed his body against hers and instructed, "Stay with Solange and enjoy the show."

Luka winked at Holly as Solange joined them. "Holly, I'll get back to you later," he whispered, pressing his soft lips on the shell of her ear and quietly added, "We still have unfinished business." And then he kissed her quickly, but fully on the lips.

She glanced away, and she was sure her face wore the flash of shock that washed over her face. But it was too late. Luka vanished into the stifling smoke. Holly dropped the vial in her purse, wondering how long Luka would let her stay with Kaine.

"That's how it is? He's quite taken with you." Solange dared to say and added with a look of caution. "Maybe as much as you are with him, wee?" She said coolly, and she didn't smile. Instead, she raised an arched eyebrow.

Again, the red sting of embarrassment burned Holly's cheeks because Solange must have seen the kiss. She wasn't going to ask, but she was sure the glow on her cheeks was like a vibrant sunset. She could try to deny it, but how could she stop her traitorous eyes that had already revealed her dilemma. Kaine's girlfriend caught kissing Luka was a harsh way to start a friendship with Solange.

Solange quickly filled in the blanks. "You're in a terrible position and don't worry, your secret is safe with me, for the time being. But let me warn you if you're planning any future with Kaine — stay away from Luka. It's obvious for anyone that sees you how possessed Luka is by you, so that won't be easy. Remember this tip. Luka always gets what he wants."

"I've noticed." Holly accepted her tip in a guilty tone. Luka's gift of energy was flashing through her body at lightning bolt speed on the heels of her sensual thoughts of him.

Solange's statement about 'how possessed Luka was by her' was strong. Maybe Solange could shed light and answer the important questions. Kaine or Luka? This was ridiculous. There was no question. There was only one answer. Kaine.

Solange took hold of Holly's hand and led her up the stairs of the giant erector set, built for the irrepressible and elusive *Hurrikaine*. Solange climbed higher up the twisted iron scaffolding to a catwalk crossing above center stage. Holly's euphoric state lent to making instant friends with Solange. They chatted about all and nothing.

"I sat here the other night and had a perfect view." Solange shared before a glut of offstage lights flooded the smoky, dismal scene below that signaled the beginning.

Holly glanced at Solange's waist length, reddish-brown hair that matched her own. As the colored light beams continued to glare, Holly noticed Solange's natural, soft, iridescent beauty. Everyone associated with *Hurrikaine* was beautiful, even the hateful Sarah in a cheap sort of way.

A sudden jerk caused the vibrations to quake through the metal scaffolding holding her. They rolled quickly at first as if to awaken her excitement then she feared the worst that the scaffolding was about to collapse. Deep inside the twisted bowels of the gigantic metal monster, a deep groan, strained to be set free and was gaining more and more strength by the second. The riveted joints of the iron construction threatened to split. A quick explosion brought a billow of white smoke. Michael hit his cymbals, simulating rolling thunder and all about her white lightning ripped jagged slices into the inky darkness. The laser light wheel started to spin a vortex, sucking, twisting, exhilarating her, nipping at her feet. The wind machine coaxed the smoke out over the frenzied crowd, fabricating the onset of a terrifying and powerful hurricane. She stared out at eighty thousand people succumbing to the anticipated arrival of their invincible leader. Thousands on the pitch moved and huddled closer to the stage chanting one word, Kaine, Kaine, Kaine.

The loud crash of a single cord resonated from Nicky's electric guitar. He held the note, forcing it to reverberate long and hard, heralding the wake-up cry. Kaine pierced the thick, gray-white smoke exploding into a billowing cloud from the center of the storm, Kaine, arrived from the eye of the *Hurrikaine.*

The crowd went ballistic.

Holly sat galvanized on the cold, hard, steel scaffolding riding out every searing crack of Michael's cymbals and cries of Nicky's blistering lead guitar. *Hurrikaine* lured her higher and higher until she heard the voice with no edges igniting her heart with a renewed depth of divine passion. Luka and her betrayal wiped from her memory. Song after song, Kaine mesmerized his awe-struck audience. Their God had arrived. His legions paid homage with all the sacrificial rituals befitting his royal status. Hail! Hail! Kaine, the Prince of rock 'n' roll, had arrived.

Kaine belted out one chart-topping hit after another.

Her body pulsated with his music, meshing as one with him while the cocaine forced its way at breakneck speed through her veins. She watched the city of fans worshipping at his feet. His nation of followers accompanied him singing his anthem, *Young Guitar Player*. And he sang magnificently and powerfully filling the arena with his soft melodic love songs as he stood center stage holding every eye.

Kaine teased the rioting fans in the front rows. He took off his coat to whoops and hollers from them. The girls jiggled their scantily clad breasts for him. He responded by returning to the center stage dressed only in his vest and fitted leather pants. The fans pushed against the crash barriers playing out a sexual frenzy, the sacred dance was peaking, promising to climax soon.

Mmmm, Holly thought, how tempting and seductive Kaine looked as he unbuttoned his vest, one button at a time and then flung it into the crowd, causing a fight to break out between the fans. The audience raged on, wild with a starvation and desperation, she'd never witnessed because Kaine took off his vest and stood naked to the waist.

She tried to understand.

She followed Kaine's animated movements.

When he reached center stage, he came to an abrupt halt with his arms outstretched crucifixion-style. His back in view of the audience and his head bowed reverently with his chin touching his chest, as a single purple light branded his head and shoulders.

The sight of him produced a fist to her gut, shaking her core foundation. She realized there, for the whole fucking world to see was proof of his undeniable sexual attraction. Holly looked on horrified, both disgusted and humiliated at the same time, as Kaine paraded his sexual gashes before his faithful congregation for their approval, sure to assume the marks to be made from passionate lovemaking.

Their hero!

Her stomach gripped her like a vice, twisting her gut instantly. "How wretched of you," she said with agony, barely hearing her words flow. The hot shot of anger flared and she was surprised because she'd never would have thought it possible to feel so angry at Kaine.

Solange leaned over and yelled into Holly's ear.

"It seems you have captured the heart of Kaine. He's showing the world he's sleeping with you. But he wants Luka to see most of all."

"You know?" Holly braved, almost too shaken to speak.

"Everyone does ... now."

Chapter Eleven

WICKED AS IT SEEMS

Holly followed Kaine. They darted into the back of the Bentley. Kaine's personal bodyguard climbed into the front seat with the driver. Holly was whisked away into the foggy night with Kaine before anyone inside Wembley realized there would be no encore.

Alone with Kaine.

It should have been blissful. Instead, Holly sensed a crisp edge.

One of them had changed.

Maybe both.

He was a different man than she had arrived with earlier. It wasn't the fact that he had changed from his stage clothes and looked positively elegant. She currently had a better picture of Kaine the performer — powerful, charismatic, and energetic. And why he'd been alone so long. Because it was exceedingly difficult for him to find someone to love him for himself. Two concerts under his belt, over one hundred and eighty thousand people had seen him, wanted him and out of all of them, he wanted her. The real flesh-and-blood of Kaine Walker, rock star, overwhelmed her.

Inside the confines of the lush Bentley, strong scents from Kaine's leather jacket and cologne oozed, mixing with the light sheen of his sweat, reminding her of a more familiar place. Kaine had yet to speak a word. He leaned forward and cracked open a magnum of Cristal champagne, poured and held a half-full glass to her lips. She followed his lead, took a sip and then he drained the glass. Kaine reached into his black, cashmere trouser pocket to retrieve a small, cylinder, glass vial filled with shimmering crystal powder.

In a flash, she pictured Luka, handsome and inviting, handing her a vial. All her guilt demons assaulted her. She squeezed her eyes shutting them tight. She must put Luka out of her mind. There was no doubt. She'd made the correct choice.

Kaine, she said in her mind to confirm her decision. She opened her eyes and watched Kaine generously filled his nose. He hesitated, leaned back, and rested his head on the back of the headrest. He closed his glassy eyes, and she listened to him make small moaning sounds of pleasure. Kaine opened his eyes.

She saw the vibrant sparkle.

She wanted it.

He looked at her. He didn't move. He sat motionless, holding the vial in his hand frightening her.

"More please," she asked under her breath. His eyes stared at her and she was unable to read his calm expression. Would he agree? His eyes said something she couldn't understand.

He made his decision, reached out to her, prepared to take her with him and liberally filled both sides of her nose.

The refresher sent her reeling, this batch more potent than the last. And she couldn't have imagined it getting any better. Holly's body continued to vibrate from the loud, pounding beat of the bass drum and her body buzzed because of the amazing cocaine. The hot blood coursed through her veins like a religious experience. She became a new convert, wanting more. And the desire started again, wanting Kaine deep inside her.

Kaine wiped tiny sweat beads from his body and hair with a convenient hand towel. He relaxed and listened to the piped-in music, as usual, John Roberts. How disinterested he seemed in his powerful performance, never commenting on the phenomenon of *Hurrikaine* in concert. Kaine Walker had somewhere else to be. He was expected. Didn't have time to experience what had just happened.

Kaine rested his head against the plush back seat, taking long, slow breaths. He wore a new, crisp, white-tailored, collared shirt, unbuttoned halfway down his chest.

His perfectly shaped chest moved with each breath sending sexual quakes rumbling deep inside her. She leaned closer to retrieve the moist towel wrapped around his neck, knowing she would soon have him.

With purpose, she set to work caring for him, patting the sides of his face dry, caressing his cheeks. She gazed longingly through his thick, dreamy lashes into his chemically charged, blue eyes that said thank you. She was falling deeper and deeper into his magnetic trance as his gorgeous face drew closer to her.

He moved to take off his jacket and then spoke. "We'll be in traffic for at least forty-five minutes." He allowed a mischievous grin.

Their eyes spoke to each other. No words were needed. Kaine's seductive performance had been over two long, torturous hours of foreplay and she was ripe for him. She needed his hands to caress her body. She needed to wipe the slate clean, set the record straight. Her choice was Kaine. She was his girlfriend, his woman, his lady, forever and always. She would wait no longer.

Her rising passion pushed her to plant a short string of kisses down the cords of muscles in his neck. Holly drifted downward and kissed the dark hair on his chest. The only sound was the tinted, window partition rising to offer perfect privacy and solitude. The growing bulge in his dark trousers told her he was ready and waiting for her. Without a word, she unbuttoned the waist button swiftly, unzipped the pants, and slipped her hand down into the moist cavern that housed the love she wanted most from him. She pushed deeper. He was harder than she ever expected.

Interesting.

The drug made him this way.

Mmmm.

Just the way she loved him. Her lips moved down the sculptured valley of his chest while unbuttoning the final buttons on his shirt to reveal his firm, rippled, abdomen. She circled the indented navel, her mouth thirsty, heading straight for the fullness of him.

Wasting no time, she slid to her knees between his legs onto the plush, carpeted floor of the luxury car. She freed him from his trousers, delighted to see him strong and slipped her hungry lips around the hardness of him. How wonderful he tasted. The cocaine pulsated through her veins, compelling her to love every inch of his velvety skin, working her own devilish magic with both her mouth and hands.

Kaine's subtle groans filled their love chamber. His strong hands ran through her hair, digging deep into her scalp, twisting long locks of her hair around his fingers. He pulled, wrapping her hair about his palms as if too weak to move and held on to her. Moments later, his pleasure escaped louder from his throat as he ripped her mouth from his hard shaft. Kaine dragged her up his chest demanding her.

"Come to me, girlfriend ... I need you, now!" He pulled her hair back to allow his lips to crash down upon hers.

She kissed him deeply, lost in the beauty and passion of Kaine, aware of nothing but their all-consuming desire.

Continuing to kiss her, Kaine leaned her back across the seat. He quickly unbuttoned the endless buttons down her dress to her waist, unhooked the front clasp of her bra, freeing her luscious breasts. He pulled away and his eyes lit with delight. He dropped searing, hot kisses down her chest, to first one nipple and then the other. He did seem to love her breasts.

She did not disappoint as the tips hardened, responding to his tongue lapping in a circular motion making the rosebud tip ache.

Nothing stopped his hunger. Kaine's hand moved down over her stomach fighting to free the rest of the buttons. When the dress lay open, her body free for his touch, with a light caress his hand dipped under the lace band of her panties. His fingers slipped on her damp skin pushing downwards and the silk cloth was too fragile to match his passion. Kaine tore them off with one deliberate motion. He briefly glanced up at her with stormy, lust-filled eyes. He checked in to see that his intense response had not frightened her again. Relieved, he hadn't, he dropped his hand down between her thighs. He placed his fiery lips on her stomach. More kisses dropped inside her thighs.

She closed her eyes, opening her legs, wanting his persuasive touch.

His brown hair fanned about, draping like dark velvet over the sides of her waist. He picked up her leg and placed it on his shoulder, the other leg lay stretched out on the seat.

Her body lay open and available for his tongue to touch her. She jerked from the bolt of lightning cutting quickly inside, fueling her lust.

He buried his head between the tops of her thighs. He sucked and licked exactly where the blaze burned freely, between the velvet petals surrounding her desire. Kaine kissed the rosebud, taking his time until she burned with liquid fire. Her hips moved with him, following him, hypnotized by him, hoping he would never stop. His hands roamed over her body, then rested under her derriere. Kaine was fiercely driven with the touch of a savage lover. Her Kaine continued to drive her to abandon. And when she arrived, there was only one word on her lips. Kaine, his name the last word to be heard.

The only sounds that filled the chamber of the Bentley were of love, woven with sighs and cries of pleasure.

Kaine erupted, releasing his passion.

She lay helpless, compelled to move closer to befriend his tongue. When he abruptly stopped and sat up bringing her beside him. She was stunned, unable to speak. Her body screamed for more of him. Her eyes pleaded. Don't stop.

He wasn't listening. Kaine reached down into his satchel and pulled a foil, turned and quickly covered himself. "Come here to me girlfriend, closer to me," he demanded. "I am sure you're tender, I will be gentle."

As promised, he gradually positioned her across his lap.

Her trust in him caused her naturally to bend both of her knees to straddle his body while he pulled the damned dress and bra off her and threw them on the floor. All she wore were her boots and love for him.

Kaine placed his hands around her waist and guided her onto his stiff love for her, in one pleasure filled moment. The sharp, piercing motion hadn't hurt, but instead, drove her wild, forcing a deep, satisfied groan that had been trapped inside her chest.

Kaine was hard, doing his best, better than his best, fantastic! His sensuous movements brought an incredible agony. Kaine slid deeper, the fullness of him an exquisite torture, filling her deep. She swiveled her hips spreading her legs further apart to take every inch of him. Passion hit her hard, deep, her lips tried to form words.

But no sound was uttered.

There was no other experience in the world to match the completeness she had when Kaine was deep inside her. A firestorm of erupting emotions continued and there was nothing in the way to stop the rush of the fire because the cocaine was pushing her, daring to blast her senses to smithereens.

When Holly's drug-laced eyes would occasionally open, she peeked out of the smoked glass window. She saw the steady stream of white, fog covered headlights. There were thousands of fans who dreamed of him in this most intimate way, 'fucking his brains out' had been the phrase Luka used. She smiled a contented smile and kissed his neck. Her naked body loved him in the manner he prescribed. Lovemaking so fierce, she expected him to tear a hole through her. But this time, she wasn't afraid, she wanted it, she was lost in the inky darkness in the back of the luxury car, falling deeper and deeper into the black hole of his love.

Shivers flooded her body like fireworks in July, again, and again, fast and slow, the maddening frenzy sent shock waves to seize her. She could no longer remain quiet and her words spilled quickly from her lips.

"Kaine ... let me go, now...."

Request granted.

With a tremendous force, he slammed her against his chest, wrapped his arms tightly around her back. Kaine rested his hands on her shoulders and pulled her down on his stiff shaft and it was like riding a bolt of lightning. She cried out, not in pain, but from unbelievable pleasure as she took the last inch of him. Blinding flashes of light blasted her to pure ecstasy as tiny sweat beads dripped from her face and fell to mix with his. Her lips dropped on his and swallowed him, sucking him dry as her body squirmed, riding out the last of him.

Kaine kissed her deep, then deeper, pushing her over, over the edge, filling her, not sparing the slightest space. His thrust was hungry, he pushed into her again, and again, to make sure, he exhausted every ounce of her passion, but not his.

She kissed him with complete devotion, lost between the seconds of time. Where would she ever find the strength to breathe the next breath?

Holly slid from Kaine's lap, a pool of liquid onto the cold, leather seat beside him.

After a long moment, Kaine removed the wasted protection and zipped up his pants. He was dressed, and she wore nothing but her boots.

She watched him rinse his mouth with Cristal champagne, then refilled. Where did he find the strength to blink? He leaned over and kissed her deeply, leaving her mouth full of champagne. Then he laid his head down on her heaving chest to rest. As her breath leveled, she ran her fingertips through his damp hair. She wove her fingers between long locks of it, pulling, and teasing.

He kissed each nipple, then suckled her breasts the way he loved to do.

He stopped the pleasure too soon, picking up her bra, helping her put it on and clasped the front. Then her dress and guided each arm into its sleeve. He took his time pushing each button through its matching hole. He loved her, took care of her. He left the dress hiked up around her waist. Then he dipped the tip of the towel into the ice bucket and delicately cleaned between her legs, deliberately sending her body mixed messages of fire and ice.

Mmmm, he felt so good.

Her magnificent Kaine was a constant contradiction, now tender and attentive, no longer the sexual animal from moments earlier. Whichever, she belonged to him.

He continued to pamper her, taking the best care of her. She could barely keep her heavy eyelids open. But he was separating the lips of her gender with his fingertips. He bent quickly and kissed her there. Just as quickly, he glanced up at her with his dreamy blue eyes, eyes that said he was devoted to her.

Fuck!

Now… she understood and nodded her head.

Seemingly, performing turned out, to be a powerful aphrodisiac for Kaine. She recalled how forceful he had been after the sound check. Finally, she'd put two and two together. If she'd understood the commanding influence the stage held over him, she wouldn't have assumed she'd been abused by him, instead incredibly loved, as she did now.

The stab of guilt was deep. Regretting she hadn't understood. If she'd accompanied him to the sound check as he'd begged. Those ugly moments in the suite would have never happened.

Kaine knew all along what he would want to do with her after he performed, what a powerful seduction it would mean.

Kaine threw the towel in the corner and helped her finish arranging her dress. He pulled her panties off the handle of the Cristal champagne bottleneck. He held the wet cloth, smiled a slow, sexy smile, and in a husky tone pointed out.

"You won't need these."

Before she laughed in response, he'd pulled her up into his arms, filled her nose with the white powder, again, and again. He dipped into the vial of sparkling crystals until satisfied.

The last thing she saw was his dreamy, blue eyes close and his champagne laced lips coming for her.

Kaine kissed Holly longingly, lovingly. Too soon, they came up riding the rush of the drug-drenched kiss. She looked around to notice that the car stopped.

Press alert!

Time for the next impossible challenge in the continuing life of a rock star. The concert, then the intimacy in the car already forgotten as they hit the sidewalk. She respectfully held on to his arm in front of the hotel.

Once again, they were delivered into the hands of Fleet Street and the paparazzi. The media broke through the security lines and attacked. Kaine's personal bodyguard fought to make a path. One particularly obnoxious reporter insisted on a quote from Kaine. His muscles tensed as she held on to his arm.

Kaine grumbled under his breath. "She is ... My Lady."

"What's her name, Kaine? Holly Hill?" The reporter shot back.

Kaine pulled Holly, heading toward the front of the elevator joining Ian and Solange. As a unified front, they tried to escape the posse of reporters.

When Solange stepped up to the waiting elevator car, another reporter sporting a different press pass caught up and cornered her. Unfortunately, he'd succeeded in separating her from Ian.

A stabbing sense of panic filled Holly. Solange would miss the jam packed elevator car. As the massive doors started to close, one bodyguard jumped out to protect Solange.

But, the door closed, leaving Solange to fight off the ill-mannered reporter. The last thing Holly heard the reporter yell to Solange.

"Who *is* the mystery lady?"

Solange answered.

"She's the *heart* of the *Hurrikaine!*"

Chapter Twelve

YOU'RE THE ONE

That was how the legend started. How Holly became known as the *Heart* of the *Hurrikaine*. She stood waiting. It was dark. A moment later, a light switched on, exposing the secret. The hotel suite was filled with a hodgepodge of famous music and entertainment personalities, each with a happy, smiling face, everyone's but Ian's.

Holly turned around and spotted Ian heading for Solange, who just arrived. He slipped up quietly behind her. Before she moved, he slipped his arms around her and placed a giant pear-shaped diamond ring on her left finger. No one heard what Ian whispered into her ear. But all suspected.

A stunned Solange spun around and stared into his expectant eyes.

"Well?" An impatient Ian asked as he went down on bended knee.

It was easy to read Solange's face, caught off guard and with a shy voice, Holly barely made out her reply.

At the top of his lungs, Ian yelled out. "She said YES!" And with that, Ian stood and picked Solange up and twirled her around kissing her constantly.

How romantic, Holly thought, recalling Kaine at the castle. Her face was beaming with joy for her new friend. Claps and cheers roared from all around the suite. Holly joined in, happy to be let in on such a special moment in Solange's life, encouraged to see a few rock stars had not discarded all traditional institutions.

Corks popped and bubbles flowed.

The next guests entered the room, Michael the drummer, with an unusually attractive blonde-haired woman wrapped around him, then behind them, Sarah.

She pinned Holly with her evil stare.

Holly instinctively slipped her hand onto Kaine's forearm for protection. He placed his hand over hers as naturally as if he were taking a breath. He continued to visit with his friend. Holly whispered under her breath. "Safe!"

Kaine switched positions and stood with his arm around Holly's shoulders. Feeling extremely loved and protected, Sarah was a forgotten nightmare.

Solange approached as if lightheaded from the excitement.

"Let me see that rock!" Holly gushed, and gave Solange her warmest smile, ooed, and ahhed, over the expensive token of Ian's love. She sighed, hoping she and Solange would become great friends. Beginnings came quickly in this crazy, fast-paced world of rock 'n' roll and the merrymaking continued. The bubbly liquids flowed. It seemed to Holly, she was the recipient of another line of sparkling cocaine carefully orchestrated by Kaine. She was on top of the world when Luka arrived.

She'd forgotten him. She didn't care. Then the reminders

arrived. Her blood started to boil because on his arm was the same beautiful woman from backstage. This time, they were causing quite a sensation. All eyes turned to them. Holly overheard a woman say.

"There is Claudine Michaels."

Holly chastised herself for, not recognizing her. Luka had been kissing, the world famous, super-model Claudine Michaels. A flush of jealousy stung her cheeks that would last a month. Claudine did not disappoint her admirers, stopping graciously to speak to them. Then turned her full attention to the handsome man at her side and slithered into Luka's arms. She kissed him with complete ownership.

Why had that sinking feeling of loss returned? A giant knot twisted in Holly's chest, somewhere near her heart, each time he kissed the beautiful woman. The dreaded feeling spread downward, becoming a pinch in her stomach. Moments ago, she'd been free. And now? Why did she care? Why didn't she stop watching Luka? Because his every move fascinated her. She watched when he released Claudine from his arms and attended to her every need. It almost looked like Luka was captivated by the woman. His eyes were dazzling.

Disappointment filled Holly, knowing he would not be bothering her again. How fast things moved in this world.

Good!

Yet, why did she feel abandoned?

Kaine's dreamy scent recaptured her thoughts. She inhaled, pushing the jealous notion of Luka away.

A deep sadness covered Kaine's face. Did he read her mind? Her hand instinctively moved to stroke his handsome face, gently, hoping she was a magician able to make his sad thoughts vanish. "What is it?"

"I realized you're going to return home soon," he complained and as if in a panic pulled her closer to him.

"You can't leave me. I've just found you."

She loved him will all of her being during that moment of confession. She smiled, having a hard time finding the right words. "We don't have to be apart for long. You will find the time, come to L.A., and stay with me." She'd hope to encourage him, wondering how she would find the time to fit him into her busy life once the new trial was in full swing. However, her invitation did not bring him pleasure. Instead, Kaine's face grew more solemn.

"No, My Lady, I wish it were that easy. I'm booked solid on the European leg of our world tour. What's worse? This is only the kickoff, not the end. I can't go anywhere near L.A., for at least three long months. Holly, please, stay with me and go on tour? Sure, it's a grind, but with me, I could show you the cultures of the greatest cities in Europe," he enticed, as his voice was becoming more excited about his idea. His face eagerly filled with joy over his obvious solution, his tongue darted out to collect his bottom lip and drew it into suck.

"No, I can't." She heard drop from her mouth. What was she saying? And to her horror, she continued.

"I have to return to L.A., for the new trial, to my home, to my life ... to reality! This isn't real, Kaine. I can't pack up and run away with you. No matter how much I'm committed to you. We can find a way to make this work." What was wrong with her? Why was she doing this to herself? And to Kaine?

A black cloud covered Kaine's facial expression as he dropped into a deep disappointment.

"But ... Holly!" He protested. "You're my lady, and you said you'd follow me anywhere." Something sinister flashed across his face as if he suddenly understood her change of heart. His eyes grew dark and stormy and the escalating hardness surprised her as his eyes pierced her soul. "Oh? I understand, Luka!"

In the same moment, Kaine was interrupted by a slap on the upper shoulder. She saw the pain wince in his eyes from her gashes carved deep into his back.

"Hey, asshole. Thanks for helping me surprise Solange." Ian blurted out to Kaine and then smiled graciously at Holly, ready to burst from his happiness.

Distracted and agitated, Kaine's jaw muscle grew taut. Kaine was not through with this conversation as he looked fiercely into her eyes and stated flatly. "Prepare to change your mind. We'll damn well talk about this later."

Kaine forced a smile for his friend and assured him.

"That's okay man, my pleasure. Maybe someday you can return the favor." He squeezed Holly's hand meaningfully.

There he went again. Had she heard him correctly? And why was he dragging Luka back into their lives? It had taken a few seconds before she became aware of what Kaine was thinking. Kaine believed she was going back to L.A., to meet Luka. He didn't trust her, and he must not believe she truly cared for him, but that somehow Luka would influence her to betray him. He wasn't far off, and she needed to prove, not only to Kaine her loyalty but more importantly, to herself. She was the one that was having covert meetings in the shadows with another man. Kaine hadn't given her one second of doubt about his commitment to her. On the contrary, he wasn't paying attention to any other women. He lavished her with affection and gifts and most importantly, his love for her. All he'd done was to create a beautiful place where they could enjoy their love. Thinking it over more carefully Holly wondered why she shouldn't go with Kaine. He was all she'd ever wanted and so much more. She'd changed her mind, he wouldn't have to, and she slipped her hand onto Kaine's arm again letting her decision settle. Soon she would tell Kaine, she would go wherever he wanted her.

Another dark moment of foreboding swept over her. She was sure Luka was involved. Again, she pushed the thought of him aside, looking up at her wonderful man, tuning out his conversation with Ian. She exhaled a deep sigh and her body responded before her mind, drawing her closer to him.

Kaine felt it too.

As if a flash of lightning brought a new thought, Kaine stopped talking to Ian mid-sentence, pulled her closer, filling her senses with his alluring cologne. He bent down, pulled her dress as far down as it would go in the back and swept her up, slipping his arm under her knees until they draped over his arm like a cloth.

He whispered into her ear. "I can't be away from you any longer."

Holly slid her arms around his neck, buried her head deep into the crook of his neck, nuzzling him, pressing her lips against his warm flesh.

Never enough.

"Coming through, please," Kaine announced loudly, marking a path through the standing room only crowd heading straight for the door.

Holly glanced back over his shoulders and shyly waved to the cheering crowd. A sea of happy, smiling faces and envious eyes stared back at her — except four.

Holly recognized Sarah's hate filled green eyes, behind her, angry blue eyes.

Luka's.

Chapter Thirteen

LIVIN' ON THE EDGE

Holly felt exhilarated. She was anticipating how soon Kaine would love every inch of her body. There was no place on earth, Holly would rather be, then cuddling in the arms of her radiant lover.

Kaine triumphantly carried her to the elevator, flanked by three bodyguards.

Was it possible, it had been four hours since the concert? With all the cocaine and champagne swirling about in her veins, the perfect place to be was safe in Kaine's arms, smelling the scent of champagne on his breath, so close to his lips. A nasty love stirred deep inside her body. All that crammed her thoughts was to have him naked beside her, loving him. She tried to stifle a tiny self-serving laugh.

"What's funny?" he asked.

"I was wondering where the satchel was?"

"Why Miss Hill, you have become the most incorrigible and sexy woman I've had the pleasure to meet in some time. All requirements to be my girlfriend, I might add." Kaine teased and flashed his wonderful bracketed dimples.

Holly kissed his lips quickly. "I'm sorry kind Sir. I find you too attractive and unable to control myself," she replied, feeling safe and cherished then nibbled on his ear near the new gold earring.

The elevator car arrived. Kaine carried her inside and allowed her to slide down the length of his body. The sparks flew like lightning riding across the top of the water. He instructed the bodyguards to take the next car, and he pushed the button to the top floor.

A few moments later she leaned into him, buzzing from another hit of cocaine he'd delivered to her. But she was truly more intoxicated with him than the expensive drug and sparkling champagne.

She slid her hands inside his coat. Her left hand bumped into something hard. "What's this?" she had questioned before he answered — though she knew.

"Protection," Kaine answered quietly dropping his lashes to hide his eyes to avoid her response. "I'd forgotten I had it on, security gave it to me when we returned to the hotel. They've insisted I wear it for the remainder of the tour. Please, no questions. It's a hazard of my occupation — the defense plan."

"Defense?"

"Yes, I'll have some defense if confronted by a deranged fan. I think it's overly cautious as if I'd have the time to pull a gun. But, easier to wear the damn thing than argue with security. Don't worry. It's nothing, seriously...." Kaine assured with a firm tone, but it didn't stop the sheepish look on his face.

Kaine carried a gun. He and Luka were gun-yielding

outlaws. Amazing! Kaine must have a good-sized one by the shape. Kaine lived an entirely different lifestyle than she had originally believed, not as glamorous as she'd always imagined because she never imagined rock 'n' roll a threat. Decadent for sure, but never a dangerous world. But it was true. Kaine placed himself in life threatening situations every time he stepped out in public or performed in front of tens of thousands. Any twisted mind might bring him down with a bullet. Hadn't Luka recently attested to more death threats?

She shook her head, knowing she had nothing to say about it. Trepidation crept inside her like a nightmare in the black, silent night, leaving her trembling, concocting horrible thoughts. Kaine could be taken from her, like Jon without any warning, anytime, anywhere. She promised herself she would not lose this man so quickly. Her blood burned with a billion tiny flames as she rubbed against him.

Kaine admitted in a low sexy voice. "I have to get you to bed."

Her body agreed, ripe for his electric touch, his fiery kisses, and the hard shaft of his love.

"Kaine," she whispered, barely able to express her drug-drenched feelings.

"Fuck! Holly, that's all I want to do," he confessed in a husky, lusty voice.

"I hope I don't scare you. But, I can't think of anything else but touching you, loving you. I want you badly..."

Chapter Fourteen

MAYBE I'M AMAZED

H olly couldn't move fast enough. She wanted to succumb to Kaine's robust charms. The material of her expensive dress tore under his impatience. She matched his zeal, removing his clothes, freeing him to love her. She sat back on her heels, smiling as she looked up at Kaine.

He stood naked, like a magnificent marble statue, a perfect male animal. His long brown hair hung over his shoulders like a cloak on a king, he stood proudly, confident, every muscle primed and ready, especially the beautiful one between his legs. The skin was stretched taut and the rounded tip was bathed with the moisture of his glistening desire. The dim light played over every ridge and valley of his breathtaking body. She rose up beside him to stand naked with him. Her clothes wrapped about her feet on the floor.

"Well, when we think alike, nothing stops us." Kaine boasted flashing his dimples.

Mmmm, it was time for bed.

Kaine pulled her beside him and picked her up heading for

the bedroom. Instead of stopping at the bed, Kaine continued into the bathroom kissing her agonizingly slow as he allowed her to drop from his embrace.

When her feet had touched the floor, he reached in to turn on the shower. Soon the room was steamy. They stood under the warm water, soaping the curves and valleys of their bodies. They devoured each other with delicious, succulent kisses lost in extensive foreplay. They barely dried off but allowed a few moments' attention to grooming and perfuming their bodies. They were preparing for a feast of bodily pleasures. It would soon begin.

Kaine walked into the bedroom first.

She joined him after combing out her long locks.

Kaine prepared the cocaine for her. He gave her what she wanted.

As the drug revitalized her body, she looked into his hot blue eyes for a moment.

He said, "We are incredibly lucky that the cocaine doesn't dull our appetites for each other."

She smiled and laughed. "Dull! I've never felt so alive. All I do is long for you. And every time you touch me, all I want is more because you feel magnificent. I never dreamed there could be so much pleasure."

He returned the smile, "I haven't begun to show you how I'll drive you crazy wanting more of me." He turned off the light. A second later the last of the moon's shadows poured thin bars of light upon them.

Kaine scooped her up into his arms and pulled her down gently on top of his long, warm body.

The drug rushed her senses. Everything in the entire world

was wonderful. The sensitive man beside her once again shed his rock star armor. His smooth hands caressed her curves, lovingly, reminding her of what pleased her. This man was her sweet lover from the castle. His lips lovingly found hers, this was the time they would finally make love in his bed, their bed, with real forever love.

The powerful cocaine rushed through her veins like electricity in a storm pushing her close to fuse her body with his.

"The satchel?" She suddenly remembered and sprang up into a sitting position.

"Fuck! See what you do to me, woman?" Kaine quickly got up and sprinted into the living room.

She saw his shaft, stand at attention as Kaine stood in a pale triangle of moonlight, searching his satchel.

His powerful erection was beautiful, pleasing to see, and made her smile again. She quietly promised, "... soon my love ... soon," as she ran her tongue across her bottom lip.

"Fuck, Holly!" he exclaimed.

"Kaine?"

"Can't we make babies?" He thundered.

Her eyebrows raised and her mouth fell open. She stammered with practicality. "I don't think the beginning of an eighteen months world tour is the time to make a baby!"

The excitement drained from his voice. "I suppose you're right. But for the record, I'd rather be making a baby."

"No!" he exclaimed again with a renewed harshness. "I can only find two more. Well, My Lady, we'll have to be creative, you up for it?" Kaine teased as he entered the bedroom.

In the dim light, she saw his eyes prancing with delight at the possibilities. Holly smiled and laughed a tiny laugh, then claimed. "I can see you are my love. And haven't I always given you what you wanted?"

"Everything, but what I want is to make a baby with you."

Holly wasn't sure what to say when he was like this. She watched his shadow cut through the edge of the darkness. A moment later, his freshly showered, lavender scent circled her. Her magnificent Kaine slid into bed beside her. His arms wrapped lovingly around her body, kissing her frantically as if he couldn't wait.

She tingled, returning his fevered kiss.

Kaine was a focused and thoughtful lover. He seemed to enjoy kissing, and kissed her long and frequently. Especially when he was inside her. That was when he loved to kiss her deeply. And when he got started on her breasts he would linger there for the longest time, with no care to be anywhere else, he made her purr. He was acutely aware not to be rough and hurt her after the sound check. But she'd survived after the concert in the back of the Bentley. Thoughts of her naked, wearing only her boots, made her wet and want him instantly and gently placed her hands on his shoulders, pushing him downward, guiding him where she enjoyed his special talent.

Kaine eagerly responded.

She awaited his arrival, bending her legs up beside her torso thrilled that he was in no hurry, but lingered. He would indulge her and she enjoyed Kaine's devotion, as he loved her, sucking and licking. Too quickly, she imploded from her toes to her head as the firestorm rushed up her spine and arched her back, slamming her knees tightly around his head.

"My Precious One."

She barely called out. A weak breath followed.

"Come here to me," she demanded pulling him.

Kaine hesitated, whispering in a deep sexy voice. "Sure we can't make a baby?"

"Not tonight." She heard herself answer between pants with a pinch of sorrow.

Kaine rustled about to protect himself. The hardness of him slipped perfectly inside her, again, and again. She quickly searched for his mouth in the dark. She was losing it fast as Kaine pumped her fiercely, pushing her closer to the edge. Holly held on to him tightly as the cocaine surrounded her climax, tearing her body apart with a promise never to stop.

Moments later she lay beneath Kaine, his weight unevenly distributed. He held her, murmuring sweet, loving images into her ear, reminding her how much he adored her. Still, he was thrusting because he never seemed to reach his climax but kept moving in her quickly and steadily.

Holly lay quiet, her body limp, like flowing liquid.

After a few moments, Kaine allowed the pleasure as he grabbed on to her, releasing, groaning, holding her, and then allowed himself to relax.

After a long pause, he moved, reached over her and grabbed the vial. And still keeping him inside her, he expertly withdrew two hits of cocaine, delivering them to her then himself.

Kaine pulled himself from her and laid back waiting for the rush. After a few moments, he tore off the spent sheath, took a small towel from under the pillow, and cleaned his hard shaft that seemingly did not wane. He turned in the shadows and tore the foil to protect himself.

He announced with an edge of apprehension. "One down, one to go."

Holly wasn't sure she could make love so soon. How silly of her, because when Kaine turned his sensual spotlight on her, she became putty to his whims and desires. Holly kissed and kissed him, tasting traces of her, deep in the folds of his mouth. The cocaine rushed, blasting her into his kiss until she lost her breath and began to pant again. He had revived her with his intense love, bringing her back for more.

Time passed as Kaine showed Holly many of the techniques and positions he enjoyed while making love. Kaine twisted and turned her body and limbs about in various ways, never satisfying his voracious appetite. He delighted her with his sexual experience, so beyond hers. Each new discovery made her happy and a willing student. Finally, Kaine entered her from behind, and his smooth, warm hands cupped her breasts. His hot, moist breath caressed her shoulder with quick short blasts. She could take no more pleasure. Without warning, deep moans slipped from her lips, his name, her words, riding her usual blazing passion as it blasted forth turning her body into a glittering pool of liquid.

"I love you." He declared, his hot lips pulling on the lobe of her ear. He frantically pushed his strength higher, searching her with quick thrusts. In a moment's time, he hesitated.

Holly moved in a slow circular motion, taking every inch of him. With one last ragged breath, she was finished. "I ... love ... you too." The words flowed from a low guttural tone, dripping from the edges of her lips. Her body quivered and shook, blasted by the blinding white-hot climax.

His back arched with hers, his lips sealed to her earlobe as he flooded her with his confessions of love, the early morning darkness their only witness.

"I love you too, My Lady, three and four times, a million times...."

Tiny drops of Kaine's sweat dropped on her cheek, cooling her hot flesh. Each instantly evaporated as he began to slip his hands over her curves. Then he turned her lifeless body over onto her back and pulled her to him running his hands all along the spine of her body.

He cradled her in his arms like a rag doll and testified.

"Wow, Holly? I feel possessed! You must be a witch and have cast a magical spell on me. I don't recall the last time I was this close to a woman, and all I wanted to do was, well, you know. How wonderful is love? And I love falling in love with you over and over again."

She smiled with complete satisfaction.

He struggled to find a comfortable level to breathe more naturally.

Where did she find the strength to whisper?

"I have a strong love potion."

Pleased the sophisticated world traveler was as knocked out by their lovemaking as she was she had to admit, he was a handful, and to keep up with him was her only challenge.

Kaine's body relaxed, his breathing even she'd thought it stopped.

"What Kaine? What's wrong?" She inquired, unable to move. She didn't want to think or worry, but he was scaring her. The knot in her stomach rose too quickly and she almost rolled up into a fetal position.

"What's wrong?" He finally addressed her concern.

"Nothing's wrong? It's, well ... I've had more than my share of, well...."

"What?"

"Women."

"Yes? Women? I'm not naïve."

Holly laughed nervously as she began to regain some ability to move. Had she disappointed him? That was it. She *was* too inexperienced.

"Yeah, women," he stated flatly.

"But Holly, I realize, I've never been truly in love with any of them before you. The kind of love we have made blows my mind. It's almost a little scary like we might ignite one of these times into this big fucking funeral pyre like in the old 60s song."

Holly smiled, yes, that song did sum up their fiery passion, and his words were sweet, comforting, and true. "You have many incredible skills. I had hoped I was getting a handle on what pleases you."

"Oh, you are! You're willing, interested, and curious. Best of all, you enjoy loving me," he reassured her.

His eyes were a dark blue and filled with lust again.

"I never thought I'd hear myself say this, I'm glad there are no more foils left in the satchel. I'd cripple myself on your fiery passion, My Lady Love." Kaine allowed a mischievous smile to curl at the corners of his lips.

They joined in a joyous laugh.

She knew what he meant, because the stirring was beginning again, the familiar warmth curled below her belly. She was no longer surprised to long for him. The need for him deep inside her. But there were no sheaths. And this was not the time to begin the family he desperately wanted.

Kaine pulled her into his warm, protective arms, her body molded perfectly to his, their love a cocoon, perfect in every way. They lay in the dark trying to calm their breathing. A few moments of silence passed in the darkness before dawn.

He whispered.

"I need you with me … you can't go back to L.A., ever."

Chapter Fifteen

HOW ABOUT THAT

Cold air rushed Holly's body. Kaine rose and popped open a couple of beers for them. He glanced at the clock while stretching his long, lean body.

"Boy, that blow is fantastic. It's late, yet I'm not tired, after all we've done. I should try a bit of a lie down." He ventured matter-of-factly and walked into the living room.

He hollered at her. "I've got to lay down tracks tomorrow, or should I say in a few hours. I'm in no shape."

"Oh, on the contrary." She corrected. "You're in excellent condition." She purred from their nest of passion.

"You're incorrigible, My Lady Love. And I love you for it. Come in here girlfriend and sit at my feet." He insisted, his face brimming with an adoring smile as she entered the room.

"Your humble servant, My Lord." She acknowledged standing naked in the doorway. She enjoyed standing naked and carefree in front of her lover. She celebrated the pleasure of the natural moment with a man, one she'd never experienced. She smiled at him. The look in his eyes said he was surprised by her blind obedience as she wandered into the room and then over to him leaning against the fireplace. He'd started another roaring fire, much as he had in her. The shadows of the dancing flames flickered on the side of his face and down the side of his naked body.

Spellbound. Damned if he wasn't a beautiful man and she appreciated that he was as fascinated with her. How wonderfully the flames reflected as if dancing on her own flesh, accentuating her curves and every move. A stabbing moment of self-consciousness stopped her.

He must have sensed her insecurity and stated to praise her.

"Holly, you have an incredibly stunning body. Centerfolds would be jealous of you. Promise me, you'll always be My Lady. I couldn't bear the thought of another man touching you. I'd have to kill him." The weight of Kaine's words hung thick in the air.

It was clear to whom he referred.

Kaine moved like a cat, piercing the fire's light to sit on the couch.

Holly took one slow step in front of the other and flicked a long curling lock hanging in front of her face back behind her shoulder. She fell into step with the soft blue's beat of Robert's guitar.

"You won't have to kill anyone, my love. I promise I will *never* leave you." Holly waited for her words to sink into his mind. She watched the spirit in Kaine's eyes grow brighter until they shone with understanding.

"You're saying you'll go with me on tour?" he offered, his tone still unconvinced. He hesitantly added. "Don't tease me."

"Yes, I will go if the invitation's open."

"Forever," he promised with a twinge of disbelief.

"Don't try to figure it out. I simply can't see myself ever leaving you either."

Kaine pulled her to him and walked her over to the couch while hugging her tightly. "I'm no fool. I'll accept my good fortune and will do everything in my power to make you happy."

"Yes, you will," she agreed. She leaned back in his warm arms, thinking she would deal with Brett, her family, and Luka another time. Right now, she was deliriously happy. She wanted to enjoy this wonderful man and her happiness. She noticed Kaine lean over to glance at the clock. She moved away to face him.

"I've got to leave in a few hours, and I don't feel anywhere near sleeping. I want to celebrate." He announced as if a light went off in his head. "Unfortunately, we're out of condoms?" He lamented, but then a mischievous smile began and his eyebrows rose.

Holly grinned.

His smile signified a surprise was on its way and his eyes sparkled.

She suggested. "How about talking? It would be nice to build a friendship to go along with our unquenchable passion. I don't have many details about you or your history."

"Talk! Talk?" He chided. "We have a fucking lifetime to talk. We only have a few good years for lovemaking while I'm still in my prime. I don't want to waste a moment of it talking, I have better ideas!" He teased, the tone playful, but unable to mask the streak of lechery growing bright in his eyes.

"No, babies ... yet!" She stated with a firm tone.

"Okay, have it your way. There are many things we can do."

"You would have to teach me." Holly moved away from his chest as he motioned to get up from the couch.

Seconds later, he returned from the bedroom with the half-full vial in his hand. "I'd be happy to teach you tricks I've learned around the world. We'll call it my global special. And to make sure I don't forget any ports-of-call, we will stay up the rest of the night."

"As much as that sounds incredible, shouldn't we try to at least rest? I'd love to give you a massage to relax you. I don't want to see you tired. Won't it affect your recording?"

"Maybe, sometimes I'm better when inspired. Who knows after a long night of loving you? And, by the way, I love the way you look out for me. Don't ever stop."

"I have no intentions of stopping. That's my promise to you." Holly vowed moving closer to her magnificent man.

Kaine stepped close, froze her nose, then his, and sat the empty bottle down on the table. He leaned over and kissed Holly long and passionately.

The massive dose of cocaine flooded her senses.

With Kaine's imagination the only limit, they started again....

Chapter Sixteen

THE POWER OF LOVE

Day 5

A golden dawn crept over the rooftops of London. Holly laid awake in Kaine's arms, counting her fifth day in London. What would happen to fill all the hours? What could possibly happen to top yesterday? They'd made love everywhere possible. Kaine confessed he wanted her with him always and then drifted into a broken, fitful sleep.

Kaine, her precious new love, was having a moment's peace as he slept. He'd awakened her with his restlessness, tormented by a nightmare. Sweat beaded on his forehead. The corded muscles of his throat were tight. What was it that crawled into his dreams to torture him? She'd placed her arm on his chest and Kaine relaxed.

Crisp, bright sun rays caressed Holly's face and coaxed her to rise. She tiptoed quietly into the living room to get a bottle of mineral water to wash the morning taste from her mouth. In the corner sat the gorgeous Gibson acoustic guitar. She wondered how many thousands of dollars it was worth as she picked up the exquisite instrument, and then hit the strings with her nail.

Mmmm, the sound was heavenly.

She set it down, walked over to the window, and pulled the curtains back a bit to reveal all of London at her feet. The marvelous view left her breathless. It was a beautiful morning to be in love. The giant orange sun was cresting Big Ben, casting a long shadow. The coolness of the room assailed her skin. She located his white shirt, unceremoniously draped across her clothes in the middle of the floor. She blushed, remembering their eagerness. She slipped her arms into the long sleeves and she inhaled the wondrous scent of him.

Holly returned to his guitar, pulled a chair in front of the window and placed the guitar on her thigh. She started by tuning the low E string and worked up each string, then wove in arpeggios until lyrics formed in her mind. She quickly searched for a pen before the words vanished as soon as they'd arrived. She grabbed a concert program and on the back began to scribble the words and feelings that rapidly poured from her mind.

"How cold I am without you in the morning's light," she said aloud shivering as she hastily wrote the words down on a program. It had been years since she'd picked up the guitar to write a song. Yet sitting here in the dawn's serene light, she remembered the music.

She sprang up again and quietly found the vial Luka gave her backstage. She filled both sides of her nose, waited a moment, until the drug did its work and refreshed, returned to the guitar.

Holly strummed quietly, reviewing basic blues chords. The quality of the beautiful instrument resonated in the quiet suite. The scent of the vintage wood entranced her. The reverberation of the music inside the guitar vibrated throughout her body. It challenging her to remember what she loved the best about music. The feelings produced by the sounds, the emotions, creating it and playing it. Yes, she understood exactly what called Kaine to the stage.

Holly sat buzzed, writing one word down after another, jotting down notes of the chords, and when she'd finished, she'd written a song for him — *Cold Without You*. A satisfying grin spread on her face, thinking, she'd bet no one wrote a song about him, for him.

The sun continued to climb into the sky. Kaine hadn't allowed this phenomenon to happen the day before when he forbidden the sun to rise, to keep her his woman. She watched the sun climb higher into the enchanting blue sky and she counted the endless sea of chimneys scatted about the rooftops.

She sat the guitar down, her fingertips burned. It would be days before calluses formed. She chugged an apple juice and wandered back into the bedroom. She stood watching Kaine sleep, filled with an overwhelming love for him. She dropped the white shirt onto the floor and slipped under the covers. She kissed his cheek lightly and wrapped up against him.

He was sound asleep, but he took her into his arms.

Chapter Seventeen

ANYTHING FOR YOUR LOVE

Holly opened her eyes. The room glowed with bright, golden sunlight. In the distance, a shower ran. She glided her hand over the cold, crumpled sheet beside her. She became aware her head was pounding in a slow rhythm. She sat up and groaned because the muscles in her back and legs ached. She tried to stand up, but her thighs screamed sit. Trapped on the side of the bed, she wondered what her next move should be.

The shower water stopped. She listened as the faucet released a gush of water, and soon the familiar sounds of Kaine brushing his teeth. With more determination, she raised herself to a standing position without wincing. She hobbled into the bathroom.

"Look what you've done to me! I'm permanently gimped." She stated, pretending to be admonishing him, then leaned on the wall and burst out laughing.

Kaine joined in laughing warm and boisterously.

She looked silly, leaning against the wall, inching along taking baby steps trying to make it to the tub.

"Good morning My Lady Love, here," he continued to laugh and picked her up high into the air. "Let me help you."

"Good morning, Precious One ... ow, that hurts too." She noted as he kissed her quickly. She moved in his arms, irritating her sore muscles, allowed a whimper to escape and then they broke into another round of laughter.

"My love toy speaks. Here, let me run a steamy, hot bath so you can soak."

"Mmmm, that sounds wonderful," she agreed with a purr, sitting on the tub siding while Kaine busied himself testing the running water for the right temperature. He dumped two heaping capfuls of purple oil into the water and soon the room reeked of the familiar scent of lavender.

When the warm water was ready, Holly held onto Kaine's hand, as she stepped into the healing water still wincing with pain. She sank deeper into the wondrous water, wondering why it was always a case of pain or pleasure with Kaine.

She leaned back in the tub relaxing and watched him shave his day's growth of facial hair. She enjoyed the simplest of routines with him, well almost. Then the room filled with his intoxicating scent.

"Where is that cologne sold? It's sooo irresistible."

"I have it made for me."

"Everything about you is specially handled."

"Everything but you, My Lady Love, I see to you personally," he verified, throwing a glance at her from the sides of his eyes.

"Yes, you do. What an excellent job you're doing."

Kaine brushed back his long, luscious brown hair and secured it in a tail. He took a quick swipe at his sideburns. He paused to file and clean under his nails and she smiled. He took amazingly good care of himself.

She studied his nude body from his ankles to the top of his head. The nakedness of him caused her to swoon a bit. Then she noticed what was missing. He wore none of the obligatory tattoo's fashionable in rock. Only the lashes of hatred and her moments of doubt scarred his perfect body. All that kept Kaine from looking like any distinguished lawyers was his foot-long length of hair secured with a black velvet cord. What concerned her were the scars left by a lash that was carved into his back. What kind of cruelty had he suffered? And why? One day she would have the answer.

"Can I help you? I can wash your hair," Kaine suggested burrowing into her dark thoughts.

There it was again, so true. The heavenly sound of his voice that fanned the heat flare deep below her belly. She nodded and handed him the shampoo.

Kaine knelt alongside the tub and lathered her long hair. He massaged her head, neck, and shoulders. Then helped her stand to rinse her hair under the shower spray and she smiled at him gratefully.

"You do take perfect care of me." She declared.

Kaine leaned down and kissed her cheek. "I've only started. I'm going to order an assortment of muffins, a platter of fresh fruits, and Earl Grey tea. Breakfast is the important meal of the day." He lectured in a lighthearted tone.

"Food? I haven't any interest in food. I, my Precious One, can live on love," she vowed, placing the back of her hand to her forehead like a dramatic actress. Then she changed her tone and rubbed at her temples. "My head is splitting — too much everything. Do you have something to numb it? And may I please have strong tea?"

"As you wish My Lady." He responded in his best Cockney accent and bent at the waist with a great sweeping bow, backed up and left the bathroom.

Holly burst into a short laugh and then protested. "Don't. It's true; it hurts my head to laugh."

Kaine turned on a Roberts CD that muffled his voice as he spoke on the phone.

She soaked, massaged her sore limbs, and then climbed out of the chilled water. She leaned on the basin revitalized, brushed her teeth, and then gingerly combed her freshly shampooed hair. Paradise couldn't be any better than this. She'd had her every wish and whim catered to, an inexhaustible lover, and a magnificent man to love her.

Holly applied a bit of mascara to her lashes and gloss to her lips. She certainly looked better than her body reported. She slipped into a white, terry cloth robe rescued from the heated towel bar. She cooed from the toasty robe. All she needed was to rest in Kaine's loving and protective arms forever.

Holly sauntered into the living room. Her muscles flexed causing minimal pain. She accepted the discomfort as a small price to pay to love Kaine and feel carefree.

To her delight, she discovered a brand new Kaine. He stood by the breakfast cart, chugging orange juice while setting a bottle of headache medicine on the cart. He wore a white, long-sleeved cotton T-shirt that hugged his chest as she wanted, a black, silk vest, and a pair of beltless 501 button-fly, dark blue Levi's. She hardly believed what she saw, noticing his white, high-top running shoes. She stifled a laugh looking at Kaine, wearing of all things a Dodger Blue baseball cap. He was perfect, except for a daring chin length, lock of dark hair that hung defiantly, in front of his handsome face. A breathtakingly, darling sight. Like a flash of lightning, the heat burned, and the yearnings started again.

"Kaine? I wouldn't have recognized you." She claimed to tease him a bit.

"Yeah, me, out of uniform," he smiled graciously exposing his straight white teeth.

Yes, she'd recognized those dimples anywhere.

He walked over close and his unique scent followed. He opened his arms to embrace her.

"I can't, My Lady."

"Can't what?" She cooed, far too happy than anyone person had a right to be. Then she tiptoed up to kiss him, the first of a thousand kisses she'd planned to lavish on him today.

"I see the desire in your eyes. And lady, it hurts me deep in my guts to tell you I can't keep you here in my arms and do the things your eyes are asking me to do. I haven't the time."

"It's started again, hasn't it?"

"Yes," he answered with a tone of regret.

"Then I'll close my eyes and dream of you loving me last night."

He must have seen a flash of fresh arousal in her eyes because Kaine slipped his fingertips inside her robe.

She opened her eyes to find him volunteering a lavish, sexy smile. The curl of a grin grew around her lips from the tickle of his light touch. Kaine's cool electric fingers moved over each breast. His thumbs flicked each nipple to instant attention and then ran his hand down her smooth stomach, causing the burn deep below her belly to boil. He had trained her body to respond perfectly to his touch. He rested his hand over her soft, mound of hair gently stroking her extremely sensitive lips, sliding between them, threatening to enter.

Holly groaned and closed her eyes, seeking his mouth, wondering if it would always be like this, his touch bringing her unimaginable, sensual pleasure? She pressed her tongue firmly between the seams of his lips, demanding entrance.

Kaine obeyed, opening and sent his tongue out to dance with hers. He pulled her deeper into his embrace as he sank down into a large chair. He took her with him and placed her on his lap, her legs draped over the chair arm, her back supported by his left arm. Kaine closed his mouth over hers and deepened his kiss. His free hand slipped down inside the robe pulling it open to give him the choice of sight or touch. He'd wanted both as he broke the kiss. Kaine cupped her breast in his hand and lifted it, brushed his thumb across the already hard nipple. He pulled at the rosy skin lightly, watching the blushing peak stiffen.

She watched Kaine's face as he touched her and the thrill when he looked up with his blue eyes darkening with lust.

No breath escaped from her, as he'd seize her nipple rendering her spellbound.

He held her gaze. "I don't want to hurt you ... you're tender." He counseled easily, his eyes full of love and concern. He relaxed, looking at her, waiting for her answer.

"I want you, Kaine."

"I don't think it will take much. I will be gentle." Kaine slid his hand up her thigh and pushed the robe open, exposing the full length of her body. He sucked in a breath, then mumbled something as his eyes feasted on her feminine form, and then added, "My Lady, what you do to me." His hand moved down to her belly, then lower caressing her. He paused a second, looking up into her eyes, then sank his fingers inside as not to hurt her.

He jerked, and the signs of an erection grew inches beneath her.

"You can feel that I'm ready for you. You won't hurt me."

She spoke softly to soothe any doubts he may have. She was already swollen, he was correct in thinking, it wouldn't take much to push her over the edge.

He smiled, but the lusty look darkened in his eyes. He pulled his fingers out and lightly traced along the soft fold.

She let go of all modestly and allowed her legs to fall open to his touch, giving him total access. She dropped her head back.

But Kaine nudged her with his left arm. "Don't close your eyes. Look at me." His voice level, and husky as he moved freely inside and outside of her touching her sensitive opening, tender from long nights of lovemaking. He circled the fiery bud with his fingertips, causing shocks of electricity to rumble inside her.

She grasped a ragged breath, swallowing a series of sighs. It was growing impossible to look into his dreamy eyes with the swirling passion rising deep inside her. She wanted to let go, to scream out, to drop her head back and let her long hair sweep the floor.

He gently shoved his fingers in as deep as she allowed.

Her head dropped backward and dangled with a deep

groan stuck in her throat.

He moved his arm from beneath her allowing her to lie across his lap like an ancient love sacrifice.

Kaine's breath quickened.

She barely sensed his chest rising and falling.

He pushed her legs further apart. One foot fell to the floor.

She couldn't move, consumed in a fiery liquid. In immediate contradiction, a cool air washed over her sensitive flesh, leaving a slight chill, knowing he was sweeping her naked body with his sensual gaze. But she couldn't move. She couldn't raise her body enough to cling to his shoulders. She couldn't stretch her arms and run her fingers through his silky damp hair, or to caress his soft, unbearably handsome face, or stroke his dreamy chest.

Kaine was gentle as he continued to slide his fingers in and out of her flowing moisture.

Her nerve endings throbbed from the hot tension radiating from her responsive and tender bud.

Kaine dropped his head to her heaving chest and caught one succulent nipple in his mouth. He circled it with his tongue and pulled at it with a hard sucking motion.

Holly shook and shuddered under his touch, the ache agonizing. It was a moment later when great waves of ecstasy washed over her one after the other, bright flashes of gold light splattered the inside of her eyelids as the suite filled with her cries of unbelievable pleasure.

Moments passed, leaving her weak as a newborn kitten, draped across Kaine's lap. He slipped his arm under her neck and brought her face close to his.

She lay limp in his arms as if unconscious.

He moved his arm quickly, shaking her, forcing her to open her eyelids heavy with his love.

His tongue darts out hungrily from his parted lips to lick his bottom lip, before the hot tip of his tongue sank inside her, filling her mouth.

She closed her eyes.

Kaine kissed the last of her senses away on a storm of erupting emotions. His rock hard intention pressed against her derrière. Coming to her senses, she barely realized it was her turn to show him attention. She shifted her posture in his lap.

"Don't move!" he demanded into her mouth with a ragged sigh, holding her tightly.

"I can't take any movement on my lap."

She opened her eyes and looked into his.

He pulled away from kissing her. "Please. Give me a few minutes, don't move a muscle," he begged as he withdrew his fingers from the wetness of her body. Then he nibbled on her earlobe. "Listen sexy lady. I've got to be at the studio in half an hour." He announced matter-of-factly while trying to calm his own breath.

"What are your plans today?"

"Well." She blurted, caught off guard, still struggling to calm her breath. She'd nothing planned other than making love with him. For the first time, she realized boundaries and time limits would be enforced, regulating their relationship. He was on tour, he was working, and she'd naively assumed she'd go with him to the studio.

"I don't have any ... wait. Maybe Solange is free for lunch though I'm not hungry in the least."

Kaine smiled in approval and replied. "Solange is a great

lady. I'd like it if you spent time with her."

"What does she do?"

He hesitated. "I forget you have little information on the band's statistics ... such a new experience for me to have to bring you up to speed on the band. She's a private detective and consultant with Scotland Yard."

"Detective? It's surprising what we have in common."

"True, she will be fascinated to learn you worked on the Collin's murder trial."

Holly sighed, "They must be deeply in love to overcome the obvious problems."

"Like we will, My Lady love."

"It must be hard with the drugs."

"No, she chose to become a private detective. That job wouldn't compromise her staying with Ian. Didn't matter, Ian stopped taking drugs. No one in the band does anymore. I stopped four years ago. Why am I doing them, again ... it's complicated. But don't let it bother you. Unusual things happen with the approval or knowledge of the authorities. You'd be surprised."

"I doubt that. I've seen corruption, more than you might expect."

"Don't worry Holly, I won't corrupt you. You and I will follow their example. We will overcome all adversity. Right?"

"Of course."

Only time would tell. It all came back to her. The reality in his world was hard and cruel and their honeymoon was over before it started.

She turned her attention to something he was saying.

"She's like a sister to me. Ian was amazingly lucky to find

her when the band first formed. She's grown up with us. I think the two of you will become great mates. What do you say about coming to the studio when you ladies finish lunch?"

"I'd love to join you."

"Okay, my love." He declared urging her to stand. The bulge in his pants vanished. He reached into his Levi pocket and held a hotel card for her.

"Here is the key to our suite. Call room service if you need anything, and I do mean anything. Sign my name."

They were ready to kiss when the obligatory knock pounded on the suite door.

They let go of each other and spoke in unison.

"LUKA!"

Chapter Eighteen

NEVER GONNA GIVE YOU UP

They laughed unison. They'd become a united front and Luka wasn't a favorite subject for either of them.

Kaine moved toward the door. His body language said it all ... Luka! Irritated with Luka's loud, persistent pounding Kaine threw open the door.

Luka pushed past Kaine without as much as a nod and headed straight to Holly's side.

She barely had time to grab a breath, let alone smooth her hair and cinch the belt of her robe.

"You okay?" he asked at once.

The smile on his face lit up the room, and his bright blue eyes were shining, seeing her half-dressed.

She knew what he was asking.

He looked over every inch of her, barely wrapped in a robe to make sure she was all right. His concern apparent as his gaze raked over her coming to a stop on one partially exposed breast. Then his attention moved down to where the robe fell open too much. His eyes were full of desire laced with restraint.

A sudden pinch in her heart said, no, his reactions were not possible at all. Luka appeared incredibly handsome. Was it possible? Each time she saw him, he turned out better looking. How did he continually manage to disarm her?

His freshly washed, scented hair assaulted her as he circled her, floated on the wind, caused by the quick motion of his movements. The hairs on the back of her neck stood with a chill, realizing he'd washed away the scent of Claudine Michaels. Holly paused, why did she care? She began to straighten the robe and pulled the collar up around her neck. She pushed those senseless thoughts swiftly from her mind noticing his casual dress.

Luka stopped inches from her. Her gaze dropped shyly to his chest. Under Luka's brown leather bomber jacket, he wore a bone colored, three buttons, beige cotton T-shirt, and a natural-colored rawhide vest. He looked scrumptious in his fitted, stonewashed Levi's. It wasn't difficult to miss how well he filled the front of his pants. The light color of blue matched his incredible blue eyes-to-die-for — the eyes that were staring at her with that confident look of, 'it's a matter of time'.

Mmmm Luka, she thought. She looked away remembering the sunburst orange baseball cap knocked back on his head with the word Texas stitched on the front making him look adorable. His thoughts clear, that if she was giving him that much thought she hadn't forgotten him. What if he was right and it was a matter of time?

Holly glanced up to see if Luka had lowered his gaze. But he hadn't. In fact, his eyes dared her to look at him. He wanted her to see how they were bursting with lust as he stood close to her, taking in his fill.

He stood too close.

His warm, minted breath blew softly across her face.

She blinked.

He was so darn cute — sexy — deadly! The combination too much and made her knees weak.

He waited for an answer. It was difficult as she fought for the words to his simple question, stunned by his daring to stand close to her. She raised her chin and stiffly stared at him straight into his blue eyes.

Calmly, she explained. "Yes, Luka. I'm fine, thank you. Though I'm worn to the bone." She let slip, trying to put him at ease, not realizing her choice of words.

"Kaine, you fucker!" He threatened, spinning on a dime storming toward Kaine. "What have you been doing to my Miss Hill?"

"Exactly what you think! And, she's not your Miss Hill, Luka. She's mine! My girlfriend, the heart of the *Hurrikaine*, the Kaine part — that's ME. Get it through your fucking thick skull!" He shouted as he pounded on his chest when he'd said 'me.'

Holly grimaced, no longer offended that she was property as Kaine reacted strongly to Luka's use of MY. Trouble was brewing again. To defuse the volatile situation, she spoke quickly.

"No, Luka. I meant the cocaine. It kept me up the majority of the night and I'm tired." Her thinly veiled remark fooled no one, especially Luka. She saw how he wanted to come to her, yet Luka was a strong man. He held his emotions locked behind a forced restraint.

Luka didn't hide the fact her words were ignored as he

reached into his pocket. "Then here's the thing." He threw a small cylinder glass bottle at her. Keep it. I've enough to keep my boy singing his bleedin' heart out all day."

Holly dropped it into the pocket of the robe.

Luka faced Kaine, his tone smooth as if they were mates again. How curious a pair they were.

"Friar Manor wants you there by ten-thirty respectively." He turned to Holly. "You, lovely lady are expected to attend on Kaine's arm. I wouldn't want to be accused of breaking up anything between the pair of you." His contempt clearly dripped with crude and sarcastic tones.

The room filled with a chill and Holly was glad when Kaine slipped up next to her. It was growing clearer by the second, Luka was not accepting her with Kaine any better today than yesterday. Though it hurt to see him with Claudine, in her heart of hearts, she secretly hoped he would stay distracted by the world famous model.

Then again, she looked at her beautiful Luka. It was always the same reaction to him. Instant sexual attraction. What was it about him that made her believe that no matter how long she spent time with Kaine, Luka would always be waiting for her? Demanding she touch him because she belonged to him.

For a split second, Luka dropped the veil over his eyes and she saw the ache, living with the knowledge she was sleeping with Kaine. It was heartbreaking to see how much he cared for her. She wanted to reach out and caress his cheek to make him understand there wasn't any way she would ever leave Kaine, she loved him and made a promise.

She was glad when Kaine pressed the length of his body

along the backside of hers for strength.

Kaine understood the moment. "Sweetheart," Kaine cajoled after he cleared his throat to break the hypnotic spell Luka cast over her. "Take this. I'll ask Solange to show you where to buy something extremely special to wear tonight." He handed her a platinum credit card.

"Oh. I couldn't." She argued and stepped forward.

"Scruples too," Luka, stated flatly. "Why don't you come to your senses? Come with me. Your good intentions are wasted on Kaine."

Holly swore she saw the hairs bristle on Kaine's neck but she too was taken aback by Luka's direct comment, especially how poisonously he had said 'good intentions.' He made her behavior sound dirty and commonplace.

Something changed. Luka was starting to fight for her. He wasn't going to sit around and wait for her any longer. Luka was coming after her. And for the first time she didn't want him to, she wanted Kaine.

Kaine pressed his body against hers. He wrapped one arm protectively around the front of her and with the other hand held out the credit card for her to take. He calmly urged. "Please, don't argue with me. Take this and get anything you want. Believe me. Money's not a problem."

Holly hesitated, understanding what he meant. But as far as the money was concerned she didn't want to feel the fine line between cared for, and paid for, therefore, she didn't want his money.

Kaine bent his head and rested his chin on her neck, whispering into her ear. "I owe you love toy because you can't walk straight."

She impulsively laughed, letting it be known they shared lovers' secrets.

Luka's face flamed with jealousy.

She couldn't stop herself as she spontaneously reached around and hit Kaine playfully on the back.

He winced but said nothing of the pain.

She suddenly experienced a sense of guilt picturing the long gashes she'd dug into his flesh.

She glanced at Luka and saw the hurt settle in his eyes as if she stabbed him repeatedly. Her laughter thoughtless in front of him with Kaine. But no matter which man she faced, she'd leave a trail of discomfort. This had to be the lowest moment in a long time. She wasn't doing anyone any good at all.

Kaine hugged her tighter, like a male marking his territory.

Luka looked as if he might haul off and smash Kaine's face.

Instead, Kaine spoke composed to help calm the highly charged air. "Put her name on the security list at the studio. She'll come later with Solange."

Unaffected by Kaine's request, Luka continued to stare straight at her. Luka took a bold step forward. So close, if Kaine hadn't been holding her, Luka would have undoubtedly bent and kissed her. She wasn't sure Luka wouldn't try again, to rub it in Kaine's face. Her heart began to pound loud, surely Kaine either heard or felt it's beating.

Kaine lets go of Holly, moved quickly and stepped between them, placing his hands on Luka's chest. He pushed him backward toward the door, almost playfully. Almost.

She relaxed. It seemed for the moment, this confrontation

ended. She inhaled Kaine's intoxicating cologne for strength, missing him already.

Kaine instructed Luka. "I'll meet you at the elevator."

Luka grudgingly took the hint better than Holly expected.

But when Kaine turned his back to Luka and took Holly in his arms, she glanced over his shoulder.

Luka produced a happy smile. "See you later." He winked and closed the door.

The burn went straight to her heart. Their strange love wasn't over by a long shot. Holly stepped away from Kaine for a second trying to read the unsettling mood.

Kaine let go of her and left the room. He returned a few moments later strapping the leather gun holster across his chest.

Anxiety leaped into her heart. She watched him slip in the shiny blue-black gun, button his vest and then put on his flight jacket. Armed — how harsh the world of rock 'n' roll. But she chose to say nothing. He appeared agitated, judging by the muscle in his jaw tensing and twitching.

"Luka woke up cranky today," Holly observed as if he meant nothing to her trying to add a bit of levity.

But Kaine, no longer in a jovial mood, turned sharply and snapped with a growling tone. "How do you know what he sounds like when he wakes up, Holly?"

She was stunned speechless.

"As I thought. Can't you see what's happening? He's tired of waiting. His feelings for you are growing stronger. I've seen him like this. It won't take much for him to misinterpret any of your actions and take advantage of you. Keep as much distance from him as you can."

"Yes, sir." She yielded and then curtsied, trying to lighten his heavy mood. "Don't worry my Precious One. I'm a grown woman. I can take care of myself. Remember, I am the heart of the *Hurrikaine*. My heart belongs to you."

Kaine didn't seem assured by her words. "Holly, Luka doesn't care." Kaine dismissed her words, shaking his head with a torrent of fury that pierced his stormy blue eyes.

"Can't you see how he wants you ... what he wants from you? It's all in his eyes, Holly ... in his fucking eyes!"

His facial expression registered disgust and then he promptly drifted into silence as if he had lost any hope of keeping her to himself.

She stood her ground. "He's alone Kaine. We have each other. Have compassion for him. He can't take me away from you. Please, don't worry."

Kaine was finished talking about Luka. "Come here, My Lady Love." Kaine grabbed her roughly and closed his arms around her, hugging her tightly as if she were a breeze about to blow away.

"Oh," she swooned and replied, "I love you when you play rough."

"I'll rough you up so you never leave my bed!"

"Promise?"

"Promise," he agreed, smiling.

She embraced him tightly and pressed her lips against his, sucking on his sweet, silky, bottom lip, already missing him. She clung a few more moments lost in a dreamy state. She couldn't lift her heavily lidded eyes.

"I love you, Holly. Please, don't change," he whispered into her ear.

"I have no plans for changing, except to love you more," she affirmed as she opened her glazed eyes.

Kaine kissed her with a flurry of short kisses.

They stood kissing, each unable to be the first to break the moment.

"See you in a few hours," Kaine finally whispered softly, weaning her from his sweet, sweet kisses. He reluctantly let go of her and headed for the door. He stopped and pressed the two fingers he had loved her with, to his lips. Then he blew her a kiss while closing the door behind him.

Holly caught the kiss midair. She stood holding it, clutching his gift to her heart. Alone in their suite, a brittle chill passed through her. The scent of his cologne hung heavy in the air.

It was sooo cold without him.

Chapter Nineteen

STAIRWAY TO HEAVEN

The phone rang. Holly wasn't sure she should answer. She set the guitar down against the chair. The ruts in her fingertips burned from the guitar strings. After six rings, she picked up the receiver to hear a pleasant surprise, Solange.

"Ian left for the studio. I took a chance," she volunteered.

"Kaine left over an hour ago. I've been playing guitar. How are you after your big night?"

"Fantastic. That stinker pulled it off, I never expected we'd get married."

"Set a date?"

"Yes, after the European leg of the tour — in California. Don't you come from L.A.?"

"Santa Barbara, initially, but now I live above the Sunset Strip in West Hollywood."

"I've been to Hollywood. We are talking about getting married in Pasadena, New Year's Eve. That's close by, say you'll come to the wedding?"

"New Year's Eve? What a party, of course, I'd be honored.

I wouldn't miss it."

"Kaine called and wants you to shop for Friar Manor."

"Sounds like fun, but I need a change of clothes. Do you have a long, casual dress because my body is too inflamed to wear pants."

"Ian is the same way after a performance. Great sex after a show is a perk in our favor."

After more womanly chatting about performance sex, they agreed to meet in a few minutes.

Holly turned around, hearing a knock at the door. After a few moments' hesitation, she answered. Relieved it wasn't Luka, but it was a uniformed man standing there holding a long, silver box wrapped with a thick, red ribbon. She signed for it, closed the door, and eagerly slipped the card out.

For My Lady
Hope you're walking soon...
Love, Sir Lancelot de Hurrikaine

Holly laughed aloud at his thoughtfulness, what a romantic man. She opened the box and there lay a dozen red roses and five white. She got the message. One white rose for every day she had known him. She hugged the box. Kaine was the best.

Another knock on the door brought Holly back to her senses. Solange whizzed past her wearing black Levi's and a black *Hurrikaine* sweatshirt that read *Lost Dreams ... Lost Illusions*, carrying an armload of dresses. "I hate it when there's no choice," Solange complained and then smiled.

Holly selected a dark paprika colored knit, mid-calf length dress. Tailored, it clung to Holly's svelte frame in all the right places. She wore no bra and panties because it was too uncomfortable from Kaine zealously loving her. She smiled. He'd kept his promise and ravished her. She gingerly sat down to put on her boots.

Solange smiled and pointed out. "Fashion will dramatically change. Kaine will insist you wear the new creations A-list designers will bring to you. It's a fun benefit of being Kaine and Ian's girlfriend. Oh, the first time I get to say it, Ian's fiancée. It's been a while since I've shopped for off-the-rack eveningwear. However, I need to stop at Asset. Let's start there. I'm sure there will be a few pieces that might work for tonight." Solange assured with a gleam in her eye.

"What's special about tonight?" Holly asked not surprised by Solange's choice to shop at Asset, considering her sophistication with fashion.

Solange's eyes flew open. "I'm glad, that for once, Kaine doesn't have business on his mind. I'll briefly tell you about tonight. You will be rubbing elbows with the purée of the music industry. It's invitation only, maybe a few lesser personalities, perhaps the younger royals.

"It's an annual charity bash, given by Sir William Larchmont. Every year a music talent is selected to honor. Tonight, your man is going to sing for his peers. Tonight is probably the peak of important nights of *Hurrikaine's* career. Every fashion plate and press hound will be weaseling an invitation. You need to look your best as the lady on the arm of the man of the hour. I suggest we get out there and shop, shop, shop!"

Holly laughed and then said. "I'm right behind you. Kaine gave me his credit card. I expect he wants me to buy something impressive?"

"His credit card?"

"Why? Has he done something wrong?"

"No! Holly, his true love for you is real. Kaine has a reputation for, well, let's say frugal when it comes to how someone else spends his money. He's generous with the band, but he's mentioned several times that women only want to be with him because of who he is and for his money. When it comes to women, he's quite jaded."

Holly swallowed a satisfying smile. He'd never been anything but generous to her. She continued to brush her recently blow-dried, long hair.

"By the way, I added you to my appointment in the hotel for a full salon treatment. It wasn't a problem at the last minute because I let it slip I was bringing the mystery woman all of London's talking about and wa-la. Everyone wants a look at you."

"I can't imagine what all this fuss is about me?"

"It might have something to do with the fact that Kaine hasn't been seen in public with a woman for over four years; not to parties or social functions. He's preferred to roam about alone. Something else might surprise you about Kaine."

"What's that?"

"I've never seen him treat any woman like he has you. The way he picked you up and carried you out of the party last night, I was stunned. As we all were. Also, he hasn't been sexually active since the tour, four years ago. He's complained and I've set him up with lady friends, but they criticized him, saying he's too self-absorbed and moody."

"I agree with the consensus, he is a bit moody but not self-absorbed. I'll have to tell you about the castle while we are shopping." She offered, smiling while she quickly thought of the highlights during all the hours of pleasure with him. He certainly wasn't alone anymore.

It was nice that Solange shared her intimate knowledge of Kaine and noted his treating her differently since Luka and Lil painted a less than positive history of Kaine and his women.

She slipped her arms into the sleeves of the *Hurrikaine* jacket he' given her. Grabbed the vial from the robe and darted into the bathroom to re-energize in hopes of keeping up with the fiery Solange.

A moment later, Holly leaned against the doorway, her head rushing. Damn, the power of the cocaine rush blasting in her head stronger than the last batch. Where did Luka find this drug? When Holly looked up to discover Solange shaking her head. Was she caught and Solange severely disapproved of drugs?

"What's wrong?" Holly asked warily, trying to keep her eyes from bulging as her head exploded.

"I'm surprised that's all."

Holly hastily prepared to explain.

"You're wearing Kaine's favorite jacket."

Holly volunteered a sigh of relief, realizing there wasn't any condemnation forthcoming from Solange.

"Not anymore. It's a gift." She quickly relayed the story how Kaine gave the jacket to her at the castle as they walked down the hall.

Solange laughed and smiled generously, then slipped her hand lightly on top of Holly's forearm to accent their new friendship.

"All of these gifts, the credit card, Holly, Kaine Walker's

finally in love. And lady, congratulations, you've done the impossible. You're lucky it's with you. It is beautiful to see Kaine in love. I never realized how beautiful he was until he met you." She spoke approvingly. Her eyes were filled with sincerity.

Holly pushed the elevator button while the potent drug swirled around in her mind and forced a confession from her lips. "Not sure if I'm to keep this a secret, but Kaine has asked me to join him on tour and I've accepted."

"You're going on tour with him is the best news," Solange announced, continually smiling. She shook her head as if the invitation verified her diagnosis of Kaine's commitment to Holly. Her full, warm smile said it all, welcome.

Inside the elevator, Solange hugged Holly warmly before she declared. "Welcome aboard the *Hurrikaine Express* and hold on its never boring."

The lobby was unusually quiet. Solange hailed a cab and gave directions. Holly spent the next three hours vigorously shopping, enjoying Solange's company as she pumped Holly for all the juicy details of her whirlwind romance and all that led up to the invitation to go on tour. Somewhere between a lingerie shop and shoe boutique, Holly paused. She cautiously asked, biting her lower lip, "What can you tell me about Luka?"

Solange eyed Holly guardedly as if asking if she wanted an answer before she submitted.

"What is it you want to know that's not obvious? He is the devil incarnate. When it comes to incredible good looks and oozing English charm, he can't be beaten. He's filthy rich, and more influential in the music industry than you'd ever imagine. He's hard-driven, ambitious, dedicated, and surprisingly loyal. Oh, yes. I'm told, a hell of a skilled and passionate lover. But who would that surprise?"

Holly must have looked taken aback at Solange's frankness.

Solange coaxed. "What is it you exactly want to know Holly?"

If there was going to be one, this moment was when she needed to confess. And if she were going to get any real insights on Luka, it would seem that Solange held the insider's viewpoint. It might help Holly understand why he focused on her.

"Since the moment I set foot in England..." she started in a quiet voice, hoping she was doing the right thing by trusting Solange. She poured out the complete magical story. How she had met Luka, fallen hard for him, other lighter details, their morning at her hotel, meeting Kaine, and how everything became twisted. That her concerns were as strong as Kaine's, having to fight off Luka. How Luka said, he was waiting for her. And the recent way Luka found a way to drive her to madness by thinking about him making love with Claudine. Lastly, how it looked like Luka was tired of waiting and coming after her; even Kaine believed that. She volunteered everything, except the extensive drug use.

"This morning when Luka came to pick up Kaine, I can't explain what he does to me, it's as if I become helpless. He controls me with an invisible power, convincing me I belong to him and always will. It's upsetting with the incredible commitment I have with Kaine. But the fact that Luka still attracts me scares me. What I feel for Luka isn't natural."

Solange caught Holly's elbow and drug her into a small Victorian tea shoppe. It was elegant, dressed with crisp, white linens on the tables, set with bone china teacups, and saucers that waited to be photographed. Rose-colored glass vases held Iris's, and three-tiered servers were stacked with scrumptious cakes and pastries. The ambiance of old-world comfort with classical music playing softly in the background. They ordered Lavender Earl Grey tea and scones with clotted crème. After their order had arrived, Solange dropped sugar cubes into her teacup, sipped, testing the hot brew.

Holly added milk, then the tea, and dropped in a cube of sugar. She wrapped her cold hands around the china cup to warm them.

Settled in, Solange leaned back and started to weave a cautionary tale. "Let's start with the obvious. You're playing with fire and you will be burned, severely. Otherwise, you've learned from your personal experience, Luka Hunter is an extremely sensual man. If you logged his sexual frequency mileage, you'd be surprised. But, as far as Claudine Michaels is concerned, she is work to Luka. He acquired the unenviable task of telling her she was bumped on the video for an unknown."

"To be clear, Luka bumped her for me."

"Yes, and she was raving mad, threatened to sue CMT. Luka's a company man all the way and he would do anything to stop her. The easiest way for him is to use his charms. He had no choice but to smooth her ruffled feathers. That's why he was attentive to her at my engagement party. It wasn't soon after you left, he suddenly had to leave her alone because of pressing business."

Holly wasn't listening anymore.

Bumped her for an unknown.

That was her! She remembered Kaine had told her Luka put her in the shot with him. But if it hadn't been for Luka, it would have been Claudine kissing Kaine in the video. Why would Luka do that? He could have kept her for himself if he hadn't intervened. Perhaps he'd placed more trust in her. Or, there was Kaine's assessment of the situation.

That bastard sat back and watched me fall in love with you, and he captured it all on film, so I would always be reminded when he took you away.

The guilt closed in around her throat and squeezed tightly. She lunged for her teacup and looked up at Solange, who had that look in her eyes as if she was about to drop another bomb. Holly closed her eyes and then opened them as if prepared, and braced for her words.

"Since you've chosen to bare your secrets, I'll tell you one in sisterhood that Ian doesn't know. A long time ago, when the band was in its fledgling state Luka and I was heading to Paris, he to visit his mother, I was returning to university. Ian and I had an ugly argument that left me fuming. Luka took me out on the town to offer a little comfort. One thing led to another, and he kissed me one of those Luka kisses you've described. I'm familiar with what you mean about the intense chemistry with him, the power and feeling overwhelmed. It can become a dangerous addiction. But from experience, I warn you, Luka is not who or what you think he is."

Kaine had said the same thing.

He is not who you think he is!

"You seemed to have overcome your bad addiction,"

Holly observed with a crisp edge that even surprised her. Because she'd been caught off guard that the beautiful Solange had been intimate with Luka, and the startling confession instantly fed her jealousy.

"I was young and very inexperienced. It took a while for me to realize what I wanted. Luka was cunning, even back then. And I did love Ian like you love Kaine."

"You're saying that Luka hasn't changed that much?" Holly asked.

"He hasn't. He is still very cunning, be very careful."

"Kaine called Luka, a tramp."

Solange laughed, to break the dark moment.

"Fair appraisal, though I don't think either man was a step up from an alley cat those days though they did clean up well. I will offer this, considering the stories you told me, the Luka Hunter, I once knew, quite well, has given up his sinful ways for creating a future with you. If it helps, AND if all things were equal, I couldn't choose between them either. Because they both have finally grown up and want the life of an adult man, with commitment, love, and family. It's the obvious problem that they're both focused on you. However, all things are NOT equal. Kaine is the better man, and I'm not saying that because he is the closest to a brother I have. I believe he's the best choice, especially since your fairy tale romance is in motion with him.

"When it comes to Luka, as I've explained, you are playing with fire. You will be burned, how severely, depends on you. I strongly recommend that you stay as far away from him as you can. Women dream of sleeping with a man like Luka every night. Well, let's be honest. He's what dreams are made of but are they angelic or demonic dreams? It bears repeating, Luka is not who, or what you believe him to be. And I'm not about to say Luka's feelings for you, aren't genuine, but has anyone mentioned you bear an uncanny resemblance to his Carrin."

"Everyone that knows Luka! Can you tell me what you remember about her?"

"What has Luka told you?" She shot back as if to knock Holly off-guard.

"Not much, a bit, their relationship ended tragically. How it tore him up emotionally."

"Well, I'm surprised he's talking about it at all. We never mention Carrin's name or anything about her, since the day she left him. If you're looking for details, you'll still have to get them from Luka. But I will venture to add one more caution. Luka has never lost anything he's wanted. I remember how he kissed you backstage. Mostly, I remember the look the two of you shared. I admit, I was curious then, but I'd never dream it had gone this far."

"Solange, I'm mixed up with everything," Holly admitted dropping her head into her hands.

"Then this is not the time to change anything. Stay with Kaine, he is an exceptional man and loves you."

"So does Luka..."

Solange sat quietly shaking her head. "It's entirely possible he does but is his love the best for you? Remember my advice and stay as far away from him as possible."

"But I'm hurting him every day I stay with Kaine. And if I leave Kaine to go with Luka, what will that do to Kaine?"

Solange shook her head and paid the bill. "I've said too

much already. I'm trusting that you will keep our conversation between us."

"Of course, I do value your friendship and words of wisdom."

But it was impossible to shake Solange's mysterious warnings. Did they stem from personal knowledge or a lingering jealousy of a romance that became ancient history? Or, was it Solange's suspicious nature, because she was a detective? Had that driven her to open up and forewarn her?

Holly shook her head. She wouldn't make the mistake of sharing her story about Luka again. There may be more women in the *Hurrikaine* camp that shared more than a passing fancy when it came to the magnetic and sexy Mr. Hunter.

As usual, she wasn't able to give the information much analysis because as Holly stepped out onto the street, the newsstand grabbed her attention. The cover of the *London Daily Mirror* read.

HEART OF THE HURRIKAINE

The letters were splashed across the top in two-inch letters.

Holly sprinted and picked up a copy. There for the world to see was Kaine, holding her hand as she followed him into the elevator after last night's concert. The picture was flattering. The article inside droned on about the reclusive Duke of Rock. It speculated that he'd finally fallen in love and quoted him as referring to her as 'My Lady' when asked who she was. It went on with an assault on his rocky past and possible future with her. Nevertheless, she was on the cover of a London paper. Inside were more insert photos. One was a silhouette of her kissing Kaine in front of the palace. In another paper, their headline read.

DUKE OF ROCK FINDS DUCHESS

This article had less damaging information. Neither paper reported her name, but it was a matter of time.

"First time in print?" Solange asked with a guessing tone.

"No, although this headline is exciting," she humbly answered, remembering all the photos of her with Brett during the Collin's murder trial. However, this time, her face took up space.

"I meant as the victim of public interest?" Solange continued, resting her hand on Holly's shoulder as if to commiserate. "Well, hold on, those bloodsuckers won't leave you alone until they have every detail about you. They're like a pack of wolves on the scent of fresh blood. What they don't verify they will make up until you don't recognize yourself."

"How much interest can I generate?"

"You're wanted, Holly."

"You make me sound like I'm an outlaw with a price on my head," she suggested then nervously laughed.

"There is. There are flyers that float amongst the paparazzi reading *Cash Reward.* Hundreds of thousands of pounds will be paid for one photo of Kaine. And more if they can capture you in the picture too. Oh, you're on wanted posters Holly, euphemistically, at least, you're wanted dead or alive."

Chapter Twenty

READY FOR LOVE

The cab was stacked full of packages, enough for three shop-a-holics. A black, ominous cloud blew in, spraying everyone with raindrops as Holly and Solange arrived in front of a bleak, unassuming building on the west side of London. The cabby graciously made five trips in and out to deliver all the packages.

Holly entered the recording booth greeted with Kaine's warm smile. He sat on the other side of the large glass window in the studio on a wooden stool. It was strange and she was fortunate to be there. That room was his exclusive territory, the recording studio.

Holly stood in the control booth, a single-track light shone down brightly. She shivered from the coolness of the booth. She tightly pulled the sash on the new leather coat she'd recently purchased at Asset. She sat down on the overstuffed, fern colored, velvet couch off to the side out of the light's dominion. She leaned back beside Solange watching Kaine do what he did best ... sing, well almost. Unusually sentimental toward Kaine, especially after her traitorous confession to

Solange about Luka, she enjoyed observing the unbelievably handsome Kaine. He sat in the soft light spilling down over his white, long-sleeved T-shirt that made him appear as if a white knight.

His chin lifted, exposed the corded muscles of his neck, straining as he sang the unfamiliar lyrics of a torch song. When he reached the chorus, he crooned in a sentimental manner.

"My Lady, my dearest Lady Love
My love for you is as boundless as the sky
And I promise to never leave you."

Holly sat back astonished. She recalled him saying those exact words to her at the castle, the morning the sun did not rise along with his promises of a new beginning.

Kaine spoke over the loudspeakers. "Okay, Ian. Last verse and we're finished."

Holly watched on with pure fascination. Kaine walked over to the piano where Ian magically worked the ivory keys. Ian pushed up his long-sleeved, black *Hurrikaine* thermal T-shirt that read *Illusions of Self* to his elbows. His long, shaggy, blond hair dripped over his shoulders. He was an exquisite looking man, absolutely stunning. Under the piano, Holly saw he wore black Levi's. Damn if all of *Hurrikaine* wasn't a pleasure to the eye.

Kaine bantered words back and forth with Ian until they fell into a pattern of the lyric.

"New song?" Holly asked already knowing the answer.

Solange whispered. "It would appear Kaine has pulled these words from his love for you."

Kaine interrupted Holly's racing thoughts. "Holly, remember the chord order I was playing the other night with you?"

"Yes, I do," she answered, wondering why he would ask her.

"Please bring me the guitar by the control booth and come sit by me."

To the side, laying in an open case, she found the beautiful Martin guitar that she'd been playing in the hotel suite.

"Bring Slick with you," Kaine instructed impatiently.

Holly shot a questioning glance to Solange.

"He means the guitar in that black case. He names all of his guitars, but Slicks' his favorite."

Hers too.

Carefully, she picked up the exquisite instrument and entered the studio. She gingerly stepped over cords and around microphone stands, sidestepping equipment until she joined the pioneering musical geniuses. The scent of vanilla hung lightly in the air from the three candles that burned on the piano. She reached out with a trembling hand and offered Kaine, the guitar.

"No. You play Slick. Please, sit on this stool." He insisted with that sexy voice of his that she never refused as he pulled the stool real close to him.

She inhaled the special scent of him surrounding her and told her quaking body to quiet down, Kaine was working and that this was not the time to make love.

He smiled at her, cocked his head to the side. His hair hung long to one side. He leaned in and kissed her, not too quickly, enough to get his fill, but mostly to put her at ease and to calm her.

He straightened his back.

"Everything is perfect." He testified, his dreamy blue eyes adoring her.

He glowed and appeared breathtaking. The sting and hot flush in her body continued as she removed her hand from his Levi-clad leg.

She needed to remember to take a breath.

Yes, love was wonderful.

He started to speak, his voice low, words floating forth quickly, but she didn't understand them.

"I want you to help me finish this song. Please, show me the chords."

Panic rose to clog her throat. She couldn't play in front of Ian, Solange, and the engineer! She was a back room guitar player and rusty at that.

"Kaine I can't. Please don't ask me," she begged grasping his arm with her free hand, holding Slick with the other. She looked around to see the surprised but encouraging looks on Ian and Solange's faces. At the edge of the darkness sat a couple of men carrying video cameras with CMT logo prominently placed on the side, patiently waiting to continue filming the documentary.

"I can't Kaine. I'm not a guitar player. I can't do this."

He bent over and kissed her ear, pulling onto the gold earring he had given her and in a calming voice said. "I heard you the other night and this morning. I know exactly what you can do. Please, try to remember," he insisted, smiled, and flashed his dimples, easing her anxiety.

This man was the one and only Kaine Walker asking and

how would she say no to him?

"Okay? Please, play along with me." He instructed and started from the beginning showing her the chords he could remember. He was so good at pulling her into his world.

She almost missed how smooth he was. Almost.

After a few wrong chords, Holly relaxed and wiped her sweaty palm on her thigh. Her fingertips burned, and it took a while to adjust to them. Soon, she and Kaine were playing in sync, well enough for Ian to join in as natural as taking a breath. She glanced at Ian and his warm smile welcomed her.

The three played together until Kaine wrote the last line of the song.

Holly drained a few beers during the session. Kaine took her down the hall to share lines of cocaine. Now, she sat listening to the playback astounded she was listening to a song not only inspired and written for her, but with her playing guitar on it. What else would Kaine make happen? Were all things possible with Kaine?

Steeped in satisfaction, she worked with Ian and Kaine until an acceptable track was recorded. She soared with invigoration, riding the gift of energy. Kaine's dreamy blue eyes were filled with a sparkling renewal. And she learned the creative process resulted in a potent aphrodisiac all by itself.

To become Kaine's muse fascinated her. Sitting close to him, he would occasionally steal a kiss, squeeze her thighs or stroke her hair. She was lucky that Kaine was an affectionate, tactile man that made love to her while he made music.

Eventually, Mo, the recording engineer, said through the speakers, "If that's it, I'll see everyone at Friar Manor?"

A time was agreed on to meet. Kaine, Ian, and Solange

stood around Holly for a few minutes, catching up on how she'd learned to play guitar from her father and how well she'd played.

Too soon, it was time to leave, another place to be.

Ian walked Solange into the booth first and over to her stack of packages.

Holly entered next and went to stand next to hers, and looked up to watch Kaine follow them into the booth.

"Good heavens, woman! What didn't you buy?" Kaine exclaimed with a straight face, his lips awry.

A stabbing guilt demon, called, "overspending," assaulted Holly.

"I've spent too much. I'll send it right back."

She bent at the waist, to pick up a stack of packages. As if her sexy posture was an invitation, Kaine's swiftly moved and placed his hips next to her derriere. He rubbed against her, as he put his hands on both sides of her hips.

He shoved his hardening hunger into her, forcing her to stand up, placing her body flush with his. His hands ran up the side of her arms to her breasts where he cupped each and began to knead them. Then he stopped, spun her around, and pulled her into his loving embrace.

She quietly placed her hands on his broad chest and the electricity flash between them.

"Nothing's too good for you," Kaine pointed out, then exhaled. He leaned close to her face, staring into her eyes for the longest moment.

She watched him close his dreamy eyes.

He flashed a great big, love-drenched smile.

"...My Lady."

He spoke admiringly and then pressed his lips to hers, hungry from all the innuendo and kisses that passed between them.

He groaned with satisfaction, taking his fill of her as his kiss deepened, then lingered.

A commotion at the door broke the kiss, much to Holly's disappointment. She peeked over his shoulder to see Solange dragging Ian over to another pile of packages.

"These are yours too!" Ian blurted out with alarm, and then suddenly aware they had broken in on a private moment. "Sorry, Kaine, fool I am to let Solange run rampant in London with my credit card."

Both men laughed as comrades. Holly joined Solange and placed another three packages on the stack.

"It is wonderful to see Kaine happy to join Ian, poking fun at a man in a relationship. He's been alone for too long."

Then Solange spoke loudly as a reply for both men to overhear. "He won't mind the price I've paid when he's taking it off me tonight."

Ian smiled heartily and retorted, "Then why don't we start at the end?"

Solange directed a wave of French words toward Ian as she pushed him out of the room with a shove.

"They're so in love," Holly sighed.

"As we are My Lady, in case you haven't noticed."

She smiled at the bulge growing in his pants, pressing her urgently.

"Oh, I've noticed." Holly agreed, as the instant thrill of hot sensations, scorched a path straight to her heart then filled her body.

Solange stuck her head in the door again.

"Sorry, last time, I promise. I forgot to tell you, Holly. Meet you at the elevator at five-fifteen to make the salon appointment." Then Solange took her leave.

They were finally alone in the control booth. Holly was thankful Kaine started kissing her again, his hands roaming up to her breasts, brushing her nipples to harden them.

Then he stopped. "Miss Holly Hill! Where are your under garments?"

"I have a surprise or two left in me," she teased with a sultry voice. She slid her hand down the front of his body, to mold her hand over the erection, growing by the inch in his pants.

"I might ask the same. Where are yours?"

Kaine stopped asking questions and kissed her.

Impassioned by his ravaging touch, she pulled him down to her. They sat on the couch and she straightened his body until his head was resting comfortably in her lap. She gazed down into his eyes that were dark with passion, impossible to resist.

"Mmmm, you smell so good," he murmured, turning his face toward her.

If she leaned forward an inch, her breasts would sweep against his face. She hesitated.

He smiled as if he'd read her thoughts. His hand reached for the bodice of her dark red dress and began to release first one button and then the next until her breasts were exposed to his sight and touch. The weight of his hand pressed against her breasts as if hungry, the tip of his pink tongue brushed along his bottom lip.

It seemed as if her breasts had grown another cup size watching his tongue, anticipating when it would devour her. She sat still, barely breathing as his lips clamped down on her nipple, hot and wet.

His tongue curled around the tip, stroking it. He began to suck, and the rhythmic pulls started a blazing path. His face with the day's beard seemed rough next to the softness of her flesh.

It made her want him even more.

The bud of her excitement was burning, throbbing in sync with the rhythmic pull of his mouth.

He pulled her closer, sucking her breast further into his mouth as if he was a starving man, and only her breast would give him nourishment. The sheer sensuality of his sucking on her breast was enough to drive her to madness. She whimpered in response. She cradled his head, her body swimming in yearning and desire.

Kaine let go, sweeping his long lashes, open for a moment.

She discovered the lustful sparkle all-consuming. "Oh, Kaine ... you're too beautiful and your warm lips feel wonderful. I can feel the want, and the..." Was all she managed.

He moved over, folding his legs more and latched on to her other breast. He repeated the motions, sucking her breast, his tongue circling and pulling on her nipple while his free hand kneaded and played with the other breast. He was in no hurry and neither was she.

She reached out with her left hand and pressed it against his muscled chest, over the ripples of his rib cage. She acknowledges with a smile, the quickness of his chest expanding and contracting with each breath. She continued her quest down to the top of his Levi's. She fought to concentrate. She unbuttoned the top button, then a second button, then a third, then a fourth, until she had enough room to plunge her hand down inside to grip the hardness of his love.

Kaine jerked and released her breast from his mouth.

"Let's make a baby," he announced then stopped and gazed lovingly up at her with those fucking Technicolor blue eyes.

"Before you say no, imagine. If we had a child, he would be a pure hell raiser. We could name him Storm," he proudly suggested in a rough, sexy voice as his hand released her breast and then groaned from her lightning touch.

"And if our child is a girl?" She queried.

"She would be Savanna after my mom, her name was Anne, and I already have a loaded gun for any young men prowling around her."

She laughed, "It would serve you right if we have all girls!"

"You say that as if we will?"

Yes, she had hadn't she.

He'd drawn her in, planning a family with her. She looked down at him. He'd given the idea of a family more thought than she'd imagined. He had his first-born's names picked out.

A grin spread across his face, too pleased with himself to get her to agree that readily.

She squeezed his sex.

"Ow! Keep doing that and we won't have any kids." He smiled.

Holly eased up and began to stroke him long and

passionately.

Kaine broke away from her grip as she said. "Would you be surprised to learn that my middle name and my Mom's name is Ann?"

"It pleases me more, it's as if destined. Our daughter will carry Ann in her name, Savanna, Ann, for her Grandmother's and her mother. But if we can't make babies, the subject is moot. And I have to stop. I don't have the satchel with me. Are you sure we can't start our family?"

"Another day my love," she pointed out in a soothing tone.

Kaine moved again turned and sat up to button his pants.

"I hate this Holly. I want to be inside you so bad my guts are all twisted with desire." Kaine stood and walked over to the engineering console, and ran his fingers through his long hair.

Holly stood and instructed. "Close your eyes."

After a moment of rummaging in her packages, she instructed, "Okay. Turn around, and open your eyes."

Holly was pleased with herself, as Kaine faced her, she watched the smile she loved splash on his face.

He flashed his dimples as his lust-filled eyes devoured her like a dying man.

She stood naked, in a sexy pose under the dimly lit track lights. She held a hand full of brightly colored lollipops. She changed her pose and then walked up close to him, and inhaled his cologne.

She'd mesmerized him.

"Pick a color."

"What are these?" he asked, still trying to calm his breath while his gaze swept up, and down her naked body. His hands reached out to touch her.

"Not yet. These, are condoms packaged to resemble lollipops. Pick a color."

He pulled a red one from her hand. Kaine's eyes sparkled with approval.

"Lady, you've graduated with the highest honors from the Kaine School of Love Making. You're unbelievable."

Chapter Twenty-One

FEELS LIKE THE FIRST TIME

L ust, but mostly love, swirled in Kaine's hypnotic, dark blue eyes. He wasn't wearing his shoulder holster or gun. He'd slip the white T-shirt off and dropped it to the floor. His long brown hair fluttered in the wind of his quick movements, settling about his shoulders. He stood quickly unbuttoning his pants.

Her eyes followed the trail of dark hair down to his last button. When she looked up into his sexy eyes, she smiled. The look said she was in for the time of her life.

Kaine reached over and flipped a switch on the console. His love song for her, "My Lady," softly flooded the control booth. Kaine reached out and cupped her naked breasts, pushing them together as his facial hair scraped against the soft skin.

Her nipples harden like pebbles as he drank with an untamed hunger.

He moved away and planted a row of light kisses up her chest, pulling her into his arms. Kaine pressed his thigh between her legs and shoved it high and hard.

The heat of his touch on her sensitive bud caused her exquisite sensations. She burned for Kaine, as he pressed against the cloth of his pants.

He put both hands on her hips and began rocking her against the denim on his thighs. "I don't want to hurt you," he whispered.

"You won't. You feel incredible." She reassured him between her shuddered moans that were growing in intensity. She sat draped across his leg, close, so close to him.

His hands kept moving her hips gently into him, in that same maddening rhythm he used with her when he was deep inside her body. He eased up, and she leaned back. Kaine picked her up and set her on the edge of the console. He moved like lightning to drop his pants down to his knees.

Holly looked down to welcome Kaine standing straight and hard, the tip glistening. She reached for the red lollipop and tore it open with her teeth and rolled it down him like she had seen him often do in the past, enjoying the strength of him. Yes, she had graduated with excellent marks. She looked up into his dreamy blue eyes filled with an urgent lust.

She whispered. "How I will ever take all of you. I've never seen you this way."

Kaine's eyes brightened, moving like liquid pools and a smile grew across his lips. His finger entered her easily as if he was caressing smooth silk.

She flowed smoothly, there wasn't any discomfort.

"You, My Lady will take me, every inch of me — I promise."

He smiled wickedly and moved closer.

The tip of him entered, gently at first, and the shockwave

reverberated throughout her body as she welcomed him. She moaned into his mouth as he penetrated her with intense power and then stopped and declared.

"You're wet, and hot, you feel incredible. You make me even harder."

Holly followed the rhythmic pace Kaine set, the male animal in him dominating her, thrusting into her as if he was reaching for an invisible paradise that called to him from deep inside her. She wrapped her arms around his back and then her boot-clad legs around his hips and held on trying to give him all the room he needed.

Sweat beaded on his forehead as he filled her again, and again, stretching her, probing her, showing her his fierce love for her. She was tired, yet exhilarated. She tried to kiss him, marking his ear with her lips because he had buried his head in her shoulder. Kaine was driven and determined this time. She wasn't quite sure why he was intense. Perhaps the love song had finally pushed him over the edge, exposing him, making him feel vulnerable. He was publicly announcing to the world that Kaine Walker was totally in love with Holly Hill, and he was telling her, and anyone that listened, how his love would be forever, and always. She would be his one and only true love.

Kaine rocked her gently, slowly, ever so slowly. His fingers delicately massaged her screaming bud until it burned. Her body was quivering with passion, growing with a fierce intensity as her legs threaten to spring out straight. But, instead, she wrapped them even tighter around his upper thighs to anchor herself.

Kaine tensed, rocking her, smoothly, then more urgently,

yet much slower than any other time together.

Holly began a succession of tiny cries of pleasure.

Kaine covered her mouth and swallowed each sound as something precious.

The ecstasy curled around her toes. She was sure he'd grown another inch. Her blood boiled, the millions of tiny bonfires returned and the exquisite torture shot up and out as her soul started to shimmer. Her body becoming liquid, claiming her, calling her to join him in a new paradise. Her body fused with his, as one soul, one powerful love. Her body quivered with long shudders as her back arched in his arms.

Kaine held onto her. He spoke quietly into her mouth.

"I love you Holly and I do mean I'm *in* love with you." His body grew rigid and with a powerful thrust, he sank deep inside her.

She clung to Kaine resting her chin on his shoulder. She struggled to rise up, straining, but there was no energy left in her. She was floating, drifting among the clouds, and then she was flying. She clung, draped across him, no will to take the next breath.

He too seemed spent, more than usual.

She fought for a complete thought, but all she mustered were two words. "Precious One."

"Fuck sweetheart, I love you. You make me a whole man. Like all this time, something inside me was always missing and I see what it was … you ... My Sweet Lady Love."

She tried to pull her head back and show him a smile and let him see the joy he alone planted there. But she wasn't ready yet and barely managed to rest her head on his shoulder as he stood straight, bringing her spent body with him, his arousal waning.

He professed, "I love you so fucking much. No one, anywhere has ever made me feel this needed, this loved ... this wanted."

She tilted her head back. She opened her love stained eyes and her gaze fell onto the small window cut into the control room door. Outside in the hall, she saw a flash of red hair. It was a blur, and moved quickly away, but not without firing a bullet of hate, shot freely from piercing green eyes.

It was hard to think.

To focus.

Kaine grabbed her derrière, pushing himself into her with one hard thrust and then held still.

"I love you my Precious One." She managed to speak in a low guttural tone. But her thoughts quickly swung back to the window.

How long had that fucking bitch Sarah been watching?

Chapter Twenty-Two

IT COULD ALL GET BLOWN AWAY

He stood dressed, looking so darn cute, not the sexual powerhouse on the stage last night or a few minutes ago. The arousal that flushed bright color into his cheeks had dimmed considerably. His entire demeanor made him look like many fraternity boys back home at the University. Kaine Walker collegian brought a stifled smile to her face, he'd been world educated.

While Holly slipped the red dress up her nude body, she felt compelled to ask. "Where's your gun?"

"Can't bring myself to defile the studio and wear it here. It drains the creativity right out of me."

She was pleased that Kaine Walker wasn't a violent man, only cautious.

Kaine walked closer and began to push each button through its matching hole. "Where are your panties?" He demanded, insisting on an answer this time.

"Kaine, please understand. My body's been ravished by a

man showing me his absolute love. It hurts to wear anything I don't have to," she explained, amused the world traveler had a conservative streak when it came to her.

"Ravished huh? Well, if you continue to have nothing but silk between you and me, I'll have you again if you don't watch out. Makes me hard to know you're naked under your dress," he said, slipping his hand around her back and lifted her up off the floor to kiss her as she slid down his chest.

"How many lollipops do you have?"

"Enough to keep you happy for a long time." She guaranteed to reassure him.

"Hopefully, that won't be long so we can start our family." He declared with a wicked grin curling around his lips.

"Enough until the time is right."

He hugged her fiercely and then whispered into her hair.

"Does Solange know all about us?" he asked in a guarded tone, changing the subject.

"Yes. I didn't think we were a secret, are we? Or, should I say ... am I? Our relationship is blasted on the front page of the newspapers. If I was, I'm not anymore."

Her face registered concern.

Kaine reacted, visibly upset by this news. "No," he maintained shaking his head. "You're not a secret. But you're news and fair game to every tabloid rag. I wanted to protect you for as long as possible. A word of warning, from this point on, make sure you're alone with Solange before you share with her, well, let's say, any private moments between us."

"Why?"

"I'll show you why!"

Kaine pulled the evening edition of the paper out of a bag leaning against the console. The cover read.

HEART OF THE HURRIKAINE
TO GO ON
EUROPEAN TOUR

Holly read on surprised. The article quoted an undisclosed source that revealed her plans to travel with the sexually explosive rock star.

"But who? How?" She stuttered as she read on in the article.

"How did they find out?" She blasted, her anger boiling over because she realized that the ordeal definitely started.

"Someone listened in on your conversations with Solange while you were shopping this morning."

"Someone followed us? Stalked us?" She stated with righteous indignation.

"You of all people counselor should understand how sophisticated surveillance technology is these days. They can listen to your conversations from across the street. And they will do worse. You always need to be on guard and careful. Stay acutely aware of what is happening around you. Suspect everyone."

"You live like this? It sounds paranoid."

"The word is cautious. Unfortunately, I'm news and it's not until you end up the butt of a reporter trying to make a name at your expense will you find out how much it can hurt. I love you. Holly, I'm doing what I can to protect you."

"You've seen the morning paper?" she asked quietly,

thinking how silly she'd been and then hoped the intruder missed her confession about Luka, especially her inexhaustible attraction to him.

"No. Ian slipped this to me when he was getting Solange's packages. Said I should read it. Why? Did you make the morning edition too?"

"Cover, in two-inch lettering, *Heart of the Hurrikaine*. Everyone knows," she said, with a diminishing twinkle in her eye. When the anger finally boiled over, she defiantly stated. "I don't care if they do. I love you and you love me, why is that wrong?"

"Our love for each other is not wrong. But it is our private business not meant to sell newspapers. I'll say it again. I'm trying to protect you from them hurting you."

He opened a drawer in the console and withdrew his holster and gun, another painful reminder that rock 'n' roll was a dangerous business. He wouldn't look her in the eyes as he slipped his jacket on to conceal his weapon.

She changed the subject and requested. "Would you be so kind as to carry these packages, My Lord?"

"Load me up, My Lady."

She laughed as she stacked the last package, covering his face and led a stumbling Kaine to the waiting car assisted by his bodyguard.

Settled in, they would not be alone for this ride.

At the hotel suite, Roberts played softly in the background, and Kaine pulled a fresh vial from his Levi's.

"Luka left it with me," he told her as he froze his nose and hers. "I'm winding down a bit," he explained, "And we've got a big night ahead of us. I'm looking forward to seeing old mates tonight. Sounds silly, but I don't get out much."

"You're right, it sounds silly," she grinned and admitted,

He continued, in a reflective mood.

Wanting to drink in each detail about him, she listened as if a captive.

"I'm like everyone else. I love my mates. During the early days, I was able to meet people and made lifelong friends as the albums took off and we climbed the charts. But fame closed in on me quickly, isolating me to the point where I seldom went out. Later, I let few new people in, mostly other musicians I'd meet while touring or my musical heroes and played with them."

"Playing guitar or singing?" She threw in quickly.

"Playing, I'm a professional man, a guitar player by trade, My Lady. I sing because the singer in the band I joined a long time ago blew out his voice, and I took his place. The rest is what you see. Everyone thought I worked the audience better if I wasn't holding a guitar. Both Nicky and I play lead guitars on our recorded tracks. Nicky and I trade off, playing lead and rhythm guitars on tours." Kaine pointed out, and then popped open a beer, offered her a sip, and then continued. "Before *Hurrikaine,* I met John," as he threw a glance at the CD player. "We struck up a friendship. Eventually, I guess it might be said I became his protégé."

"John Roberts!" She blurted utterly astonished and impressed.

"Yeah," he emphasized and in a humble tone, "I guess, as they say, the rest is history. By the way, you'll meet him tonight."

"Tonight is a big shindig, isn't it?"

"Biggest shindig, as you call it, of my career. Since I can remember, Sir William has thrown this annual charity bash to spotlight a band or musician. It's for the music community to show support. Tonight is to acknowledge that the band has climbed to the top of the heap. The last few years I've been invited as a guest in the audience, but I still can't believe that tonight the spotlight is on the band. It's been twelve long years in the making. The old, overnight, took a decade, success story."

He paused and made a quick visit to this mysterious thoughts. He half-laughed and offered resolutely.

It's been even longer trying to find you. I have everything I've ever wanted to happen to me. Come here, girlfriend."

"With pleasure," Holly obeyed and swayed up close, oh so close.

"It's four-fifteen when did you need to meet Solange?"

"In an hour," she muttered, looking hopefully into his eyes.

"Time to pick a color?" She shamelessly suggested and smiled, letting him see she was ready for him again.

"You, My Lady, know what I'm thinking. You're a witch, plain and simple." Kaine accused and then granted her a devilish smile.

"You're not that difficult to figure out, but I need a bath before I leave for the salon. I couldn't muss up a thing on me when I get back. I must look my best for you tonight."

"You know how I like you, naked, making wild love to me," he stated.

"That would start the tabloid's tongues wagging if I showed up dressed only in my love for you."

They laughed and Kaine kissed her.

Holly broke away much sooner than she wanted.

"Last chance, let's soak in the tub."

She led him into the bathroom. There she prepared the bath water with lavender scented oil and slipped off her dress. She turned to him, letting him take his fill of her.

"Coming?"

"Oh, I intend to, sweet lady," Kaine stated flatly. He turned on a portable CD player sitting on the bathroom counter and popped in the blues singer Richard Cobble.

"I'm going to get us beers."

Kaine quickly returned with two beers, a lime, and a fat candle. And, of course, he set the vial down, lit the wick, turned out the lights, and started stripping in front of her.

Mmmm, his firm chest rippled with each movement, and she wondered if she'd ever tire of seeing him undress. He unbuttoned his Levi's, one button at a time. Ordinary, yet sexy, like an exotic dancer, and then dropped them to the floor. He stood naked before her, he was gorgeous ... and she breathless. No, she would never tire of him.

He reached for the vial and took care of both of them. They stepped into the tub. He sat, pulling her to sit in front of him.

There she laid back, relaxing, waiting for the rejuvenation while listening to the wounded Cobble warning about losing everything.

They drank beer, occasionally washed a leg, or thigh, breast, whatever was closest.

Mostly, it was wonderful for Holly to relax and listen to his heart beating.

"Must be close to your meeting with Solange." Kaine finally reminded when the CD finished playing.

"I don't want to leave you." She purred contentedly.

"Go ahead, My Lady. I have a few things to attend to before we leave." He instructed, leaning her to one side and kissed her neck.

"Keep that up and I'm not going anywhere," she chided as a playful challenge.

"Go ... before you can't," he gently commanded.

Holly stepped out and picked up a towel.

Kaine spoke, almost in a whisper.

"Wait, a moment. I want to look at you one more time."

Chapter Twenty-Three

SEVEN O'CLOCK

K aine's blissful, blue eyes lovingly caressed her naked body. It was an incredible moment knowing the sight of her pleased him.

"May I leave?"

"Yes...." He trailed adding a sad face.

She glanced down at him, walked over, bent to sit on her haunches. She leaned over and kissed him sweetly, hoping to cheer him up a bit.

"I won't be long, I promise." She caressed his face. To be separated from each other, for short amounts of time, were becoming more difficult.

Holly hurried into the bedroom and slipped into a long, pale-yellow, cotton dress of Solange's. Grabbed her *Hurrikaine* jacket, threw the key card in the pocket along with a vial and rushed out the door hoping she hadn't kept Solange waiting.

Solange leaned against the wall when the elevator doors opened.

"I'm sorry, waiting long?"

"Can't tear yourselves apart? Good sign."

Holly entered the lavish spa off the lobby of the hotel. A small battalion of manicurists, makeup artists, and hairdressers stood beside a masseuse.

"We're here for the works," Solange announced.

The works it was: facials, leg, and brow wax, manicures, and pedicures. Their hair was styled and finally, make up applied. Holly's long wavy hair was curled up with falling trendles. By seven o'clock, she was ready.

"Can I interest you in a making music video mademoiselle? I'm not without influence." Solange teased when she came over pleased to find Holly transformed into an elegant, and sophisticated woman. "I see why Kaine has stopped his wandering eye. He'll be delighted. Let's go. I need time to fuss."

Holly was refreshed and feeling pampered, and well taken care of, but mostly loved by Kaine. He did want the best for her, and it showed.

Solange leaned over and warned. "Per Kaine's instructions, a quick media lesson. Every eye is going to be watching you tonight. Remember, other than last night's concert, he hasn't arrived at any public event with a girlfriend since the early years. Stay with him, hold his hand, and as antiquated as my instructions sound, speak when spoken to, because he's a professional and aware of exactly what words to use, to protect both of you from the press. Follow his lead until he says it's time for you to wait for him. Please don't be offended, he is doing it for you because he loves you. You'll sit with me and the girls, it's what we do."

There was a Rock Star Girlfriend 101 after all!

Solange and Holly entered the lobby, heading for the elevator. The paparazzi swarmed into the lobby.

Solange quickly instructed. "Don't say a word. I'll handle everything."

Holly nodded in agreement though she'd had enough experience with the Collin's murder trial. She realized she'd never spoken about her media qualifications to Solange. Oh well, it didn't matter, it was time to meet the press. The crowd pushed in on Holly, worse than she'd ever experienced. She inched toward the elevator. This time, they were looking for her and the barrage of questions assaulted her.

"Are you Kaine's mystery woman?"

"Are you *the* Holly Hill from the Collin's murder trial?"

"You come from L.A.?"

"Are you fucking Kaine?"

"After all Kaine's hard drinking and heavy drug use can he still fuck?"

Holly stopped. The disgust flashed across her face and she turned before Solange stopped her screaming. "How can you ask such filthy questions?"

Solange pulled frantically at Holly's arm. Alarm covered her face. "Come on, Holly, keep moving."

The *Hurrikaine* security team arrived to assist them, clearing a path to the elevator. Safe inside, Holly leaned against the car wall and sucked in a few good breaths. "How can they ask me if I was fucking him? How could they?" Holly raged, more angry than disgusted.

"The rags can, and will ask worse than that," Solange reminded.

She was wanted dead or alive. She was like him, subjected

to scrutiny, and that was how he lived. What was she getting into with Kaine?

The doors opened on Solange's floor. Holly cautiously peeked out.

Solange smiled approvingly at her pupil. "You're getting the idea. Always check if anyone can see or listen to you. Ian's concerned, the bands concerned, hell we all are, because you and Kaine, are the hottest item in London. Remember, the rags will pay hundreds of thousands of pounds to get an exclusive with Kaine's elusive mystery woman. We all have a strong protective feeling for you. Please understand, because we have all been where you are. Well, none of us has been dropped into the pot with the water boiling as you have. Lastly, per Kaine, expect the press will crash Friar Manor in disguise, pretending to be a friendly, interested guest. Be careful. Watch whom you speak to and what information you divulge. They are extremely cunning."

"I'm not sure about any of this, Solange."

"You're happy with Kaine. That's all that is important. You're strong, Holly. That's why Kaine has fallen in love with you. He knows better than anyone does what your life with him will mean. Only a few of us have survived. But he has faith in you that in spite of all the problems that complicate his fame that you will handle it or you would not be here."

Solange was right. She'd always been exceedingly careful with information during the trials. One leak would lose the case. Soon she would have to tell Solange, she did understand. Still, it was terrifying as the focus of the ruthless press.

Solange continued her instructions.

"Sounds medieval, but remember to smile and say as little

as possible."

Solange hugged Holly briefly for support. "Ian and I won't be forgotten by the press, our engagement has been timely. But I'll do my best to stay near you if you need me. It can get treacherous coming face-to-face with Kaine's fame. It's been the most remarkable and powerful force in his life, that is until he fell in love with you."

The elevator door started to close as Solange stepped out. She reminded. "Ian and I will ring about nine-thirty so we can arrive fashionably late."

The doors closed.

Holly shivered as the chill settled in, and her friend left her to her thoughts. She pressed penthouse, exited the elevator, and said good evening to Kaine's bodyguard perched there.

Holly stood outside her door waxed, rubbed, scrubbed, massaged, and styled. One of the world's wealthiest men pampered her. She was Kaine Walker's woman, and she was trembling, scared by this realization.

How long could this possibly last?

Twenty-Three

FOREVER MAN

The first thing to draw Holly's attention was his tall, lean, silhouette in front of the backdrop of a blazing fire. Kaine spoke in a low voice on the phone with his back to her. The CD player blasted a quieter Roberts. She glanced to her left where she saw a fresh dinner cart decorated with three lit candlesticks. The ice bucket held a champagne bottle with the nose pointing to the sky. A plate of leftovers told her Kaine had been nibbling. A platter of sliced chicken and a crystal bowl filled with leafy salad waited for her.

She realized she hadn't eaten anything since the tea shop but she wasn't hungry. She picked up a slice of chicken, and a bite of shredded carrot. No, taste. Positively not hungry. She felt obligated to pecked at the appetizer plate of dry, tasteless food. However, her mouth rejected it, and instead, demanded a drink to quench her dry as a desert palate. She checked to see if the refrigerator was restocked.

"Counselor, wait. I have a few surprises of my own." Kaine enticed, dressed in luxuriously tailored fabrics. He wore a silky, long-sleeved, crème-colored dress shirt, buttoned to the top ending at the straight collar. He'd layered with a charcoal, worsted-cashmere waistcoat. The shirt, neatly tucked into a pair of baggy yet tailored, charcoal colored, cuffed-trousers made of the same vest material, no doubt handmade from his personal Asset collection.

Surprised again, she smiled accepting his choice of footwear, black, suede, capped-toe shoes. His dark, shiny hair, hung long and loose, falling softly over his broad shoulders. A few arrogant strands draped near his chin line. What an elegant man!

Kaine hung up the phone and moved toward her with the grace and posture of a well-bred man.

Her heart skipped a beat, trying to understand how she had found him. How long would it take her to accept the fact that Kaine Walker was all hers, a talented musical genius, elegantly dressed, devilishly handsome and such a sexy man to love forever?

"Well, aren't you an exquisite picture of beauty?" He complimented raising his arched eyebrows suggestively.

"You're not doing bad yourself, my love, you're absolutely gorgeous," she cooed while his magical cologne hovered about her luring her to him.

"Is it all right to kiss your lips?" Kaine teased.

"When it's not, I'll go away."

"Don't ever tease about leaving me."

His eyes blew with an intense fury she had seen only once before at the castle. He took her in his arms and his warm, champagne-laced breath blended with hers.

"You tempt me My Lady Love, with your charms, beyond

what is humanly possible," he whispered, his words meant to send a flush of heat throughout her body. He leisurely kissed her evoking delicious, sinful, responses from her.

Holly sent her tongue into his warm mouth. She explored at first, with a gentle motion until she met his tongue and it was like electricity. The growl of desire rumbled from deep within his chest.

His hands dropped down and clasped her bottom, hungrily kneading the mounds. He pulled her tightly against him, his hardness alerted her he was ready for love. Kaine kissed her passionately and it's power squeezed a tear of joy from her eye. He opened his dreamy lashes and looked down into her face.

With half-lidded eyes, she gazed up at him to see his alarm.

"Did I hurt you? I'm sorry if I did." Kaine apologized breaking the kiss.

She placed her finger to his soft, moist heart-shaped lips.

"No, my love, you didn't hurt me. You loved me."

"Holly ... my love, we are extremely lucky to have found each other."

"Indeed, we are incredibly lucky."

"Tonight is a special night of celebration. I have a couple of surprises for you. Go, get dressed and I'll have them ready when you return. No peeking," he added mysteriously.

Holly quickly retreated into their bedroom and closed the door. She discovered Kaine had her meager possessions hung neatly beside his in the closet.

Excited, she pulled out her final daring purchase. A low cut, black, sheer body stocking. She slipped into the built-in thong, pulling the clinging stocking up over her erect nipples, covered with black, intricately embroidered lace that showed the full curve of her voluptuous breasts, but covered her nipples. A thin, sheer material enclosed her arms to her wrist, and the bareback plunged into a dramatic V-effect.

With great care, she pulled up her thigh high, black silk nylons and then picked up another box with a pair of black, velvet, Prada platform heels. She stepped into them as she caught a glimpse of herself in the full-length mirror. She was stunned; this reflection wasn't Holly from the starchy, conservative law firm. This woman was a fashion forward seductress, once created by Luka now taking on a life of its own. She shook her head in disbelief, laughing aloud until she thought the tears would streak her eye makeup.

It had been another incredible full day with Kaine and the beginning of what she expected would be an unforgettable night. She walked over and dabbed on an absolutely ridiculously expensive perfume called Joy, Solange insisted she buy.

It will be worth it when he's kissing every place you put it to drive him crazy, Solange promised and smiled wickedly.

His impatience blasted from the living room.

"We've twenty minute's tops and I have something for you," he winked and smiled generously.

Holly kicked off the heels, hurried into her black Asset, stovepipe tuxedo trousers, and pulled them up over the body stocking, sucked in her tummy, zipped them and then stepped back into the heels. She hoped her outfit was not too daring and revealing to suit her surprisingly conservative world traveler. She sucked in a breath for courage and cautioned.

"Here I come, I hope you like this."

He called out. "I like you best naked, the rest is icing," he reminded sweetly.

With a long sweep of her arm, she grabbed her new floor-length, black leather coat, a small black evening bag and opened the door. Suddenly she inhaled the rich bouquet the scent sooo familiar. She filled the doorway, searching his face for a favorable response.

But she was surprised by his expression.

He stood still and his mouth opened a bit and released a long breath.

As her gaze moved on to sweep the room, a smile burst across her face as she turned her head. The room was filled with roses.

He'd done it again!

His intense stare caught her eye, and they locked on to each other.

"You don't like what I'm wearing," she was quick to criticize. "Damn, this bodysuit is too revealing," she said and turned away.

"No!" He yelled then lowered his voice. "Don't move," he demanded.

After a moment's hesitation, she looked in his eyes. But what she saw was how much he adored her, and there hadn't been any better moment in her life.

"Is this my beautiful Holly? The lady I love more than anyone in this world?"

She relaxed and let down her guard. "Possibly, depends on what you think?" She admitted trying to hide her insecurity, but in her defense, she'd never dressed this provocative. After all, tonight was Kaine's important night. She wanted him proud of her.

"I'm impressed. Let's see. I had no idea you were into the raging new styles."

"Don't forget I went shopping with Solange, but that's not fair. I found this, and she encouraged me. Do you approve?" She invited scrunching up her face, waiting for his response, remembering this world was his.

"Well," lifting his hand to curl about his clean-shaven chin.

"I think something is missing."

"You mean the bra?" Her face flushed with the heat of embarrassment.

"Of course ... I have one."

"No, I love the bare effect on you. You don't need support there. But something *is* missing. Come to me girlfriend, and model for me."

Intrigued by his suggestion, she began to walk like a runway model, in step to the upbeat music, turning, and swirling, leaning forward, twisting, and showing him her bare back.

He whistled, applauded, and made sexy sounds.

She loved his attention.

"Come here sweetheart, I do have something for you," he coaxed with a full mischievous grin.

"What more can you give me? Look at all these beautiful roses. I'm the happiest woman alive Kaine Walker. And it's because of you."

Kaine retrieved a tiny purple velvet box from his waistcoat pocket.

She held her breath. This couldn't be what she thought it might be?

"Open it." He quickly ordered with all the enthusiasm of a young child at Christmas.

Stopping at the couch, she dropped her coat, and bag and began fumbling, anticipating its contents. Could it be a ring that soon?

Cautiously, she popped open the lid and found a single diamond. Upon further inspection, it was not a ring but a single stud earring though the stone was much larger than the five karats in Brett's engagement ring.

"Oh, my!" She cried out overwhelmed by his generosity. She looked up at him trying to keep her composure.

"This is too extravagant. I can't accept this."

"Sure you can and will. Nothing is too good for My Lady Love. And soon to be the mother of my children. Let me help. I called my jeweler yesterday and had him create this expressly for you. Let me place it in your ear."

Holly looked up and swept her hanging trendles to one side for him.

He bent and kissed her neck below the shell of her ear saying.

"Mmmm, you smell wonderful, good enough to eat."

A grateful smile crept over her face as she made a mental note to thank Solange later.

Kaine took out her right gold hoop, and then on the left lobe, he exchanged that gold earring with the diamond stud.

Holly slid her arms up around his neck and whispered.

"You're perfect, and you're mine."

The thought to kiss him was irresistible. The flames of

love descended on her with ease, like lightning cutting into a storm cloud. She pressed her lips next to the fullness of his hard, demanding, mouth and her tongue caressed the seam of his.

He parted his lips.

Hungry for him she dove inside, and the kiss ignited an explosion inside her, followed by a series of fiery eruptions, exposing waves of raw needs. She craved Kaine, knowing she needed to satisfy this lusty, desire — or explode.

He groaned with pleasure from her impassioned kiss. Her arms slid around him tighter, drawing him closer. She molded her body to fit his, pressing her hips into him.

His growing sex teased her and fell into a natural, rhythmic motion as old as time itself.

Her eyes opened to find his locked onto her lusty gaze, and all she wanted to do was make love with him more than ever. She pulled his hair back away from his neck to kiss him and to her delight, found a mate to her stud earring, the giant diamond shined brightly in his earlobe. She kissed it as Roberts crooned in the background.

Kaine spoke above a whisper.

"Diamonds are forever ... and so am I. Let's have a glass of champagne girlfriend and a freeze to celebrate you're staying with me and going on tour. Tonight has been another dream of mine. To find you, My Love, and then see the great cities of Europe."

Kaine kissed her quickly on the lips as he patted the mounds of her derrière. Kaine broke away and poured the champagne.

A slow stroll around the room allowed her to admire each

vase filled with dozens of beautiful, fragrant red roses. She looked up to find him intently watching her. She smiled with amazement. There was no other man like her magnificent Kaine.

"It's all for you, My Lady. To show you how happy I am too. We are extraordinarily lucky to have found each other."

She ran into his open arms.

TO BE CONTINUED...

Dear Reader,

Please take a moment and leave a few comments about your favorite scenes wherever you purchased **DEVOTED**. It is crucial to the series to have immediate feedback while the pleasure from the story is fresh in your mind. Thank you for your valuable support.

YOU ROCK!

A disillusioned woman...

Holly Hill followed her heart and her fairy tale world is better than any she could have imagined. But is she in danger of that world crumbling?

A frustrated man...

Luka Hunter, a rock music executive, is tired of waiting for Holly.

A charismatic

Kaine Walker, lead singer for the rock band Hurrikaine, greatest dreams have come true. He has everything he's ever wanted, but for how long?

Has Holly made the right choice?

Did she love the wrong man?

Find out in BETRAYAL (Part 5) London

http://www.kewtownsend.com/

KEW TOWNSEND

Affairs of the Heart Series ~ London

HEART (Part 1), *TEMPTATION* (Part 2),
PROMISES (Part 3), *DEVOTED* (Part 4)

Forthcoming:
BETRAYAL (Part 5)

Ms. Townsend is a widow with a wonderful daughter, educator of school-age students, travel and movie buff, and writes romantic music fiction set in the 1960s-1980s rock scene in the *Affairs of the Heart Series*. She lives in sunny Southern California and loves to read under a palm tree with wave's crashing along the shoreline.

KEW's love of rock music began at a young age when she returned glass Coke bottles for change to buy 45 rpm records. Her interested moved from the music to the musicians, and living in Hollywood, interviewed the Beatles when they landed at Los Angeles International Airport. Acquiring a taste for the funny Englishmen, she began dating one of the Rolling Stones that exposed her to sex, drugs, and rock and roll. Later her memories surfaced in the *Affairs of the Heart Series* where she weaves her behind the scenes anecdotes with her long love of castles, mysteries, lightning, and thunder into a romantic suspense story. Her master's degree in Cultural Anthropology and Archaeology adds to her world travels, and flavor to her novels.

CONTACT KEW

kewtownsend.com

Leave a message, a review, and sign up for NEWSLETTER. Be first to hear about new releases, preorders, sales, prizes, giveaways, and fun events.

www.ingramcontent.com/pod-product-compliance
Lightning Source LLC
Chambersburg PA
CBHW030323180626
46810CB00003B/1206